THE WALL
CAME TUMBLING

THE WALL
CAME TUMBLING

Larry Galvin

To order additional copies of this book, contact:
Xlibris Corporation
1-888-795-4274
www.Xlibris.com
Orders@Xlibris.com
82638

For the *love of money* is the root of all evil.

—1 Tim. 6:10

Introduction

The U.S. banking system is probably the largest, the most advanced, and the most complex ever devised. Its complexity also makes it the most fragile. Its entire structure is held together by one thing and one thing only—the confidence held in it by the public sector. Without that confidence, the U.S. economy implodes upon itself. The stock market crash of 1929 is a perfect example, caused by nothing but the panic of investors on Wall Street. There were no major earth-shattering events which occurred prior to that fateful October day—no earthquakes, no tsunamis, no terrorist bombings of world financial centers in New York, nothing. There was only panic.

The Banking Act of 1932 was enacted to address many of the problems resulting from that catastrophe, but one fact still remains painfully obvious—less than 4 percent of total deposits in this country's banks, savings and loans, credit unions, and other depository institutions are actually held in the form of cash. The other 96 plus percent are invested by those institutions in the forms of loans and other investments to earn money. To allay some fears of the public as January 1, 2000, approached, the Federal Reserve printed over $500 billion in order to just stave off a feared potential run of depository institutions should computers crash as we entered the new millennium.

Most people alive today never experienced the Great Depression, and we cannot begin to understand what our parents and grandparents must have gone through. The Roaring Twenties was a period of unparalleled prosperity. The "war to end all wars" had been won, and everyone was enjoying the good life. And then, in a matter of days, Eden became hell, millionaires became paupers, and as is true today, when the U.S. sneezes, the rest of the world catches a cold—in this case, a severe one. The culmination of the October 29 crash was the rise of Hitler and Mussolini to power, World War II, and the deaths of over 65 million people.

President Reagan, against his wishes but with pressure from a liberal Democrat-controlled Congress, signed the Tax Reform Bill in 1986, which had the result of devaluing real estate and ultimately causing the collapse of thousands of banks and savings and loans (over two hundred in Texas alone). I worked for the FDIC in Houston, Texas, from 1989 to 1993 at the peak of those closings as both a paralegal and account officer in charge of collecting on judgments of those failed banks, and so I have intimate knowledge of some of the things that occurred there in late 1989. An investigative reporter for ABC, Wayne Dolcephino, obtained some confidential FDIC documents from an FDIC employee, which suggested that there was a mole within the FDIC leaking information to certain unscrupulous people of upcoming bank foreclosures. *I know this for a fact* because the bank file in question, Resource Bank, was in my office when the person got ahold of its contents. Anyway, the management of the FDIC blew its proverbial gasket when the story was aired in the Houston area on channel 13 although, to my knowledge, the culprit or culprits were never brought to justice. Mr. Dolcephino's investigation took him to some people near Salt Lake City, Utah. When he asked the man who answered the phone if he could interview him regarding certain bank failures in Houston, Texas he was refused entrance into his property. While this story might appear innocuous at first, it allowed a certain criminal element to infiltrate many of our banks. They would do so by approaching a failing bank's board of directors prior to its collapse, buy out the shareholders for only pennies on the dollar, set themselves up as the board of directors, make a series of fraudulent loans to fictitious companies that they had created, pocket the money, and then vanish, thus leaving the bank in much worse shape than it had been by the time it was finally shut down. The stated tab to the American taxpayer was a $165 billion bailout that Congress passed in 1990, but that was not the final cost. The governing body of the savings and loan industry (FSLIC) was also forced to close. It was eventually replaced by the Reserve Trust Corporation (RTC). Their losses were even greater because most of their assets were tied up in real estate investments.

Author's note: Remember that this is a book of fiction, of course. But *what if, just what if* some person (or persons) could actually infiltrate a bank's depositor base on a massive scale and steal their money? And what would it do to the confidence of those depositors if it indeed happened? Of course, due to security measures put in place by banks, nothing of what you are about to read could ever actually take place because no one could ever actually hack into your bank accounts and steal your money. So again, don't worry. The book *is* fiction. Your money is totally safe.

Preamble

August 6, 1945 (8:15 a.m.)

Four-year-old Mitsuru Obah and his three-year-old sister, Michiko, were playing happily in their aunt's small front lawn on the swing set their parents had just recently purchased for them. From their viewpoint on the slopes of the nearby mountains, they had an excellent view of the entire city where their parents had left for work three hours earlier. They were both far too young to understand anything concerning current events, and neither had any idea that there was conflict in the world. Their parents had gone to work, and they would soon return—it was that simple. Mr. and Mrs. Obah had asked his sister to look after the children as the war began to ebb into the annals of history. They dared not speak openly of their opinions as to the outcome of the war for fear of drawing the ire of their fellow workers at the factory, although it was apparent from their expressions that they could see it too. *The Emperor is too blinded by his pride and the words of his commanders to face the inevitable. The Americans have demonstrated their ability to strike at the capital of our homeland with impunity. Plus they have total confidence in the war's outcome, and now we have nothing to fight them with. How many more deaths of our citizens must we endure when they attack our coast and our homeland? Yes, we will continue to work though the bombs may start falling on our factories and though we know it is a lost cause. But you alone must bear the guilt and the shame you have brought upon us.*

The front door of the tiny house opened as Mitsuru and Michiko's aunt stepped out to check on her young charges. Having heard the drone of a single multi-engine plane overhead, she was concerned because planes flown by her countrymen rarely took place anymore, since it was imperative to save fuel in order to prepare for the upcoming invasion. Reassuring herself that all was peaceful, she turned to go back into the house when a sudden blinding light appeared in the middle of the city below. Moments later, a strong gust of wind

11

knocked the three off of their feet as it hurtled up the slopes. The flimsy home flipped over on its side like a collapsing deck of cards. Seconds after that, an equally strong wind caused by the enormous suction of the blast came rushing back down from the mountains. Their aunt finally struggled to her feet and checked on the boy and girl. Seeing that they were safe, though somewhat dazed, she turned and found herself gazing upon the most horrific scene she had ever witnessed. Her beloved city, as she remembered it, no longer existed. Fires were burning everywhere, and above all, a huge mushroom-shaped cloud was beginning to grow.

Chapter One

1988

Inside an inexpensive hotel room in Houston, Texas, two men waited patiently beside the telephone. Unlike their drab surroundings, they were dressed in tailored business attire, one with a briefcase. They had just finished breakfast at a nearby Denny's restaurant, and after returning, they had changed from the ordinary work clothes they had been wearing and placed them in a plastic trash bag. Had anyone been able to listen in on their conversation they would have immediately noticed a distinct east European dialect.

The phone rang, immediately cutting off their discussion. The one in charge of the briefcase picked up the receiver and listened for a few moments before replacing it in its cradle. In perfect English he told his compatriot, "We need to make a visit to Resource National Bank. I'm sure its board of directors will be interested in what we have to offer them."

1993

In the bathhouse of one of Tokyo's exclusive business communities, a small man with a white towel wrapped around his waist, opened the door to the steam room. Billows of steam enveloped his body, and he immediately inhaled deeply, letting the heat fill his lungs. It was lunchtime, and he often took this opportunity to escape the rigors of his high-profile position. Finding a seat in the corner, he sat down and leaned his head back against the wall, closing his eyes briefly. It was only then that he became aware that there were no voices to be heard in the room. That's unusual, he thought to himself, opening his eyes and looking around. Except for him, the steam room was empty. He shrugged and closed his eyes. He then heard the door to the room open and close quickly, followed by the sound of two pairs of footsteps approaching. He opened his eyes once again and suddenly, through the heavy steam of vapor, two men stood before him. "Mr. Obah," one of the men spoke in Japanese, although he was clearly not of Far Eastern descent. "My employer would like to have a few words in private with you."

Present Day

Manuel Constanza stood up through the opening of the limousine he was riding in, smiling broadly at the large group of people cheering and waving at him. It had been a brutal campaign. The election had been nasty with both sides hurling personal insults and charges of corruption at the other (not uncommon in Mexican politics). Now that it was over, Constanza was confident he could accomplish much in the area of reconciliation, reform within his government, and mending ties with their neighbor to the north.

The United States had shown considerable interest in the political situation brewing in Mexico and had expressed pleasure that a pro-US official had been elected since the alternative had been a decidedly left-wing Marxist. However, resentment toward the United States was now reaching epidemic proportions because, as Constanza knew, an apparent about-face had taken place by Washington DC regarding the NAFTA agreement. So much opportunity for an economic stimulus to his country had been riding on it.

Now, instead of remaining home, thousands of his countrymen continued to stream across the porous border daily in Hudspeth County, Texas, just east of El Paso, to escape the poverty they were trapped in. Security in the United States was so bad that the flood control dams across the Rio Grande River were routinely traversed by large vehicles containing not only illegals but large bags of marijuana, cocaine, crack, heroine, and many other illegal substances. If border agents happened to be watching these points of entry, the drug dealers would get that intelligence from their people on the American side of the border and simply drive their trucks across the shallow points in the river as there were not enough agents to cover all the points of entry.

Many decades of being forced to deal with rampant corruption of Mexican politicians at both the national and local level and the brutal violence of the many drug dealers on both sides of the border left millions of Mexicans feeling that there was no other choice but to pay coyotes huge amounts (by Mexican standards) to sneak across. Many Americans living in the border towns were too frightened to leave their homes. Many others, angered by what they felt was unfair treatment of Hispanic people who had fled across the border, were calling for their government to formally default on the billions of dollars it owed to the United States. Constanza had tried to assure the U.S. government that no such action would ever happen while he was in office and that he would do his best to stem the illegal flow of his people. His first official act had been to ask the United States for a moratorium on the interest payments due to America's largest creditor banks in New York. Without it, he pleaded, it will be impossible to rebuild. Under pressure from the comptroller of the currency's office, the money-center banks had reluctantly agreed.

As the presidential motorcade proceeded down the Reforma, past the U.S. embassy and the boisterous crowds, a shot rang out from one of the nearby buildings. The bodyguard sitting inside the limousine immediately grabbed Constanza's waist and pulled him inside for protection. He needn't have wasted his time. In the middle of Constanza's forehead was a small, circular hole. In the back of his head, a much larger exit hole left no doubt as to the fate of the president-elect. Outside the limousine, pandemonium reigned.

* * *

Within the thick-paned glass doors, the room was cool and sterile. Access to the room was only attainable by a few employees using a credit card in conjunction with the correct use of a five-digit code on the keypad affixed to the wall. There was little conversation being conducted among the four individuals inside as each was absorbed in his or her own job duties. It was nearly 2:00 a.m., the graveyard shift. The only sounds emanating from the enclosed space were quiet hums of the large computer hard drives. Along the walls were tall machines containing magnetic tape discs, spinning briefly, and then stopping before continuing.

A cell phone from inside the pocket of one of the technicians gave a faint buzz against his waist. When he answered it, a voice with a thick accent came over the line. "Is everything in place?"

"Yes."

"And you are sure this can be done." The silence of disgust could be heard loud and clear. After a brief pause, the line went dead.

Replacing the phone inside his pocket, the technician walked, largely unnoticed, to a nearby unoccupied console. He removed a 3½ disc from his pocket, placed it into the empty drive, and then hit Enter. Three times he repeated the procedure with new discs, and as quickly as he had begun it, the operation was complete. The discs were returned unseen to his pocket. The tech then picked up his cell phone again, hitting the number 8 followed by Talk. Voices came on the line. Speaking quietly, he gave all those who were listening a series of instructions to be inputted on the other end. He then disconnected his phone again and looked down at the console. Looking around to make sure he was unobserved, he hit the Enter button one last time. There was an almost imperceptible drain on the bank's electrical power as the lights inside the room briefly flickered. Things immediately returned to normal. The other three technicians glanced up briefly at the lights and then went back to what they were doing. At six other locations, similar occurrences were taking place.

*   *   *

The dacha was located just south of Moscow's city limits, approximately fifty yards from the main road. However, the shrubbery surrounding the building made the building virtually invisible to any casual passersby. Additionally, the tall wrought-iron fence would help ensure the confidentiality of the meeting about to take place. The cars used to summon the visitors were parked well out of sight in the rear, leaving no outward appearance of anything out of the ordinary.

The hallway entry remained relatively quiet despite the presence of the six men standing in it. The last had just arrived moments before. All of them wore suits, although none of them were businessmen. They were, in fact, former high-ranking officials in the KGB—*former* because all had been part of a failed coup to dislodge Putin from power several years previously. Most had been caught and seriously dealt with, and only six remained. All had a price tag upon their heads, and Putin's spies were everywhere. To be apprehended meant immediate incarceration and execution.

A set of double doors at the far end of the hall opened, and a handsome young man in military uniform, save for the jacket, stepped out. His shirt and pants were neatly pressed as if just from the cleaners, and he moved with the air of one who had undergone a lifetime of military training. He wore the rank of captain on his shoulder epaulets, and the other six men recognized him as the aide of the man who had summoned them.

"Please, comrades," he spoke in a precise military tone, "come in."

The men walked into what appeared to be a large study or private library, still without speaking, and approached a round table situated in the middle. Inside the room, thick curtains were drawn to prevent outside light from penetrating. However, a sufficient amount was being provided by the overhead fixture. The décor revealed the tastes of one who obviously possessed great intellect, judging by the number and variety of books that stood on the shelves of the mahogany bookcases occupying three walls of the room. A closer inspection, had they elected to perform one, would have revealed to them volumes of books in the fields of philosophy, science, history, and religion. The Bible, the Book of Mormon, the Koran, and materials from all the other world religions were there.

After the last man had entered, the captain closed the doors and spoke to them again. "Comrade Kheraskov will be joining you shortly. In the meantime, please help yourselves to the food he has prepared for you." He motioned to the center of the table which held two platters, one heaped with small sandwiches and the other a coffee dispenser. Before any of them had thought to ask a question, the captain closed the doors behind him, leaving them alone in their silence.

One of them finally spoke up. "I do not suppose, comrades, that any of you has any idea as to what this meeting is about any more than I do." The voice belonged to Alexander Musorgski, the tallest of the group.

"Well, it is obviously more than a social visit," came a wry response from the man next to him. "Otherwise, we would be having more than coffee to drink, don't you agree?"

Several chuckles were heard over the comment. Kheraskov's affinity for fine wines and vodka were as well-known as his penchant for beautiful women.

"I suppose we can all agree on that point," Musorgski nodded. "I suppose we will simply have to wait for an explanation. Until then, I am rather hungry."

With that comment, he, like the others, fell on the food before them.

A few minutes later, the sound of increased activity from beyond and the opening of the front door caught everyone's ears. One of the six walked over to a draped window, pulled back the curtain, peered out, and motioned the others over.

A Zis limousine could be seen stopped at the front of the iron gates. It momentarily waited while unseen eyes verified the vehicle's identity through a small camera set inside the stone pillar.

Had the rear windows been down, the car's occupants might have been able to barely hear the soft buzzing sound that preceded the opening of the iron gate on silent, well-oiled hinges. The car then proceeded up the gravel pathway past a huge immaculately manicured lawn, finally stopping in front of the house. The driver, dressed in a well-tailored suit, emerged from the car. Only an expert with a trained eye would have noticed the slight bulge underneath his right arm—and the men inside were all experts.

The captain who had admitted them appeared from the front door of the house as the driver opened the rear door of the vehicle. A third individual emerged from the back seat, wearing, despite the heat outside, a full-length gray coat and, more conspicuously, a pair of black riding boots. He turned around and reached his hand into the car, and a beautiful young woman stepped out. Another figure, with only the back of his head visible, remained in the car. The man in the coat and riding boots leaned over and spoke to the man in the car, then turned, shook the captain's hand, and briefly exchanged pleasantries with him. The two men and the woman ascended the steps to the house, leaving the driver to attend to the sedan with the other individual remaining inside.

Inside the entry, the woman paused briefly and smiled at her companion. "Please do not take too long," she said.

"I will try to be as brief as possible," he replied, "but it may last two hours or more. And I promise I will make it up to you. This evening, we will go back into Moscow for dinner at the Bulvar, and then we will attend the ballet afterwards."

The woman appeared disappointed before turning and ascending the circular stairs. The man stood for a moment, watching her as he slowly unbuttoned his coat. Underneath, he wore a general's uniform.

The most noticeable feature of the general, the uniform notwithstanding, was his face. It appeared as if it were chiseled out of stone, making his blue eyes stand out even more and drawing attention away from his slightly thinning hair.

The captain spoke, "They are all here, Comrade Kheraskov."

"Good."

The double doors to the study opened again as Kheraskov strode purposefully into the room. The six inside dutifully stood in respect to the one who had once been their leader as the top man in the Russian spy organization.

Kheraskov walked over to the desk at the other end of the room and laid the gloves in his hands on it. He then turned his attention back to the men behind him.

"Good morning, comrades," he boomed in a voice that sounded oddly upbeat. "It appears you have been enjoying the food that was prepared for you. I trust that none of you had any problems in getting here."

"None whatsoever, Comrade Kheraskov," answered Musorgski. "We are all, however, a little intrigued by your invitation. Perhaps you would care to enlighten us."

"I have always liked that you want to get to the point, Alex," Kheraskov laughed. "Therefore, I will waste no time in getting to the point of our meeting. I have brought you men here to discuss the future of our country."

Eyebrows were raised.

"The Soviet Union is dead," came a low voice. "The Berlin wall has fallen, and our attempts to remove Putin failed. Now we are being hunted down like rats."

"We are not finished yet, Oparin," said Kheraskov evenly. "However, if any of you feels like Dobzhansky, I will not think less of anyone who chooses to leave now, although I do not think you will."

Silence fell upon the room briefly. Dobzhansky's pessimism was understandable, yet all of them were aware of Kheraskov's reputation when it came to matters of his beloved homeland. If he had summoned them to discuss the country's outlook, then he obviously felt there was a good reason behind the meeting. No one left the room.

Kheraskov spoke up again. "Your attempt to dispose of Putin was admirable," he said before adding, "but poorly conceived. Had you come to me beforehand, I would have advised against it, at least at this time."

"Why?" asked Musorgski.

"Because you failed to take into account the one factor that must be present in any successful revolution, which was present in 1917. You did not have the support of the people on your side. In fact, despite the current economic woes that we are still facing, our people still remain solidly in favor of the ongoing attempts to turn us into a democracy. Your efforts were doomed from the beginning."

"Then what are you suggesting?" Musorgski inquired. "That we somehow turn public opinion in our favor?"

"There will be no further need to turn the masses against Putin. Initially, I had hoped that this meeting would not be necessary, but it appears that our former KGB friend likes his current position and the power at his disposal too much to desire any change. It is therefore incumbent upon us to facilitate the change ourselves."

"But if the people want capitalism, then how is what you are saying going to change things?"

"I submit to you that the people do not know what they really want," replied Kheraskov. "But you are missing the point anyway. Putin is a Gorbachev puppet. He has no more of a chance of succeeding than Yeltsin did. Gorbachev began something he could not possibly finish. You cannot have part communism and part democracy together. It must be all one or the other. I believe the American president, Abraham Lincoln, said it best: 'A house divided against itself cannot stand.'"

There was a brief pause.

"The economy," he continued, "is the single most important part of the equation. As long as current economic policies survive, so will the current political situation. But if something were to happen that would cause the policies to significantly fail and the economy to badly deteriorate, the people would demand change."

"But the Americans keep lending Putin billions to keep the Russian economy from sinking," Dobzhansky complained.

"My dear Oparin"—Kheraskov smiled—"you have just provided yourself, and the rest of us, with the answer to the dilemma."

Everyone looked perplexed for the moment. Then Musorgski raised his eyebrows.

"Do you mean you are going to stop the Americans from giving us the money?" he asked.

"Exactly," stated Kheraskov. "If we can stop the flow of money from the West, capitalism in this country cannot possibly survive. With the mafia, the gang activity, and the terrorism that currently exists, our fearless leaders are unable to do anything about it. The people thought they wanted freedom, but if they cannot see positive changes, they will demand Putin's head, and we will be there to pick up the pieces."

"Your reasoning is logical," said Musorgski skeptically, "but I do not see how we are to convince the Americans to stop sending him money. And when is your plan to go into effect?"

Kheraskov picked up a remote control device off of his desk and turned on a nearby television. When it had warmed up, it turned out to be a news broadcast. The picture displayed a scene of chaos with a news anchorman talking about the assassination of Manuel Constanza.

"It already has, Alex. I made an important call a short while ago, and twenty years of hard work is now being played out. The time is now perfect. America is now just starting to rebound from its own troubles with their mortgage crisis and their huge bailout of it. If we can somehow give them a little push over the edge, their economy will crumble like a house of cards. And now, I would like you to meet someone who is going to help us do just that. His name is Mr. Obah. He cannot stay long and has brought along his interpreter, but I am sure you will be highly interested in what he has to say. After that, I have one more little card to play that I will tell you about that will occur on the twenty-third of this month, just to ensure our success."

Chapter Two

Elaina Grigoriev walked upstairs and into a small bedroom that had been prepared for her use. On the bed lay a tray containing some toasted raisin bread, cream cheese spread, and a butter knife. Elaina had pretended to pout a little but, in truth, it had provided her with an opportunity she had been hoping for. On an earlier occasion when they had been in the general's study, he had had to excuse himself in order to attend a need in the kitchen regarding a small problem that dealt with the evening meal. She had pulled a small listening device from her purse and affixed it to the underside of his desk. For weeks it had remained unused, but now it appeared there was an opportunity to intrude upon his privacy.

Elaina was the headstrong, twenty-four-year-old daughter of a Soviet politician. After spending two years at the University of Moscow, she had cajoled her parents into allowing her to continue her studies in London (a decision which her father, a staunch communist in his own right, often regretted). While in England, she had completed her major in economics. But while she had been studying Keynes and Galbraith, the CIA had been studying her. During her three years, CIA operatives had infiltrated her classrooms where they had engaged her in a number of study groups. They had planted seeds of discontent with the state of Russia's economy where Elaina had come to see the disparity between the free market economies in the West and the miserable failure of Russia's stifling communist system. She had learned one basic tenet why communism would never work in the real world—human nature. The concept was a very simple one: if you gave an individual an incentive to produce more and a reward to be successful and better himself, he would do it.

Elaina fit the CIA profile perfectly for a number of reasons. First of all, she was unhappy with the economic plight of her beloved Russia. Second, being the daughter of a high-ranking politician, she had access to places that a typical young woman did not. And third, she had one other trait that few other women, especially in Russia, possessed—beauty. By Western standards, she was that rarity among Russian women. Her attractiveness would often turn the heads of men walking in the opposite direction, and in simplistic terms, she could be described as no less than stunning. The CIA wanted that—needed it. After all, beauty and sex were not avenues to power only in the West.

It had been a long, slow process. The nurturing of her natural dissatisfaction with the situation in her homeland had been the easy part. However, convincing Elaina to use her beauty as a means to gain access into certain circles had been a more arduous task.

Elaina's training was thorough, but her handlers were content to bring her along at a slow pace, not wanting to place her in an environment that could be dangerous and risk losing a potentially valuable asset that could be worth even more at a later date. They told her that first she was to learn to be aware of her surroundings and, when in the company of politicians, to listen in on any casual conversations within earshot. If she proved adept at it, future training would always be available. Headstrong as she was, Elaina fumed with impatience over the deliberate pace.

The perfect opportunity to ingratiate herself into the right company had presented itself shortly after her graduation from the London School of Economics and Political Science. It came in the form of a diplomatic social function that her handler had arranged for her to attend. Her instructions were simple, accompany her parents and allow herself to be proudly displayed by them to their friends and others in attendance. If matters worked out to her handler's expectations, further instructions would be forthcoming.

Among the attendees at the social function had been Dimitri Kheraskov, director of the KGB. Attracted to her beauty, he had latched on to Elaina almost immediately and spent the majority of the evening monopolizing her time.

Elaina was not initially attracted to the man, being thirty years his junior, but she had allowed herself to be courted because of who he was. She soon learned that pursuing a sexual relationship was not his primary goal. On the contrary, he seemed simply to enjoy having his ego boosted by being seen in the presence of beautiful women. In addition, he proved to be quite intellectual, and soon, the disparity in their ages became less important.

When she next met with her handler, she was given a miniature listening device that was attached as a working part of a cell phone. He impressed upon her the seriousness of what he was giving her and told Elaina she was only to detach it when she was sure she could not be detected. While she was thrilled at the opportunity of being given the chance of using it, he also made it clear on the consequences of being caught. He told Elaina once she had planted the bug in a safe place, she should then tell him so that he could, in turn, activate it. That would ensure that no random electronic sweep of the area could detect it.

* * *

It was about three in the morning when a private phone rang inside the residence. The man inside awoke and picked up the instrument on the nightstand beside his bed. He listened briefly to a voice then sat up immediately and hung up. He had scarcely replaced the receiver when, seconds later, the phone rang again.

* * *

Closing the door behind her and removing a small receiver from her purse, Elaina fit the earpiece to her ear. Adrenalin was flowing through her at an enormous rate as she listened in on the conversation taking place below her feet. Notepad out, she was ready to take down anything she felt might be important. She took her bread knife and spread some cream cheese across the toast, but as she continued listening, she forgot about the food in front of her. She began writing furiously when, all of a sudden, the door burst open, and she found herself staring at the cold eyes of Kheraskov's lieutenant.

"What are you doing?" he demanded.

"I-I'm just listening to the radio," she stammered.

"Then you won't mind if I listen in, will you?" he sneered. "I want to see what station you are listening to."

"Of course not," she replied, pretending to stand up in order to hand him the headset. As he got to within a couple of feet from her, Elaina felt a wave of panic come over her and tried to bolt past the man. He was too quick for her, however, grabbing underneath her left arm and spinning her around. Until that moment, Elaina had forgotten she had not let go of the butter knife still in her right hand. Although not particularly strong, fear and adrenalin gave her strength. As she whirled around, Elaina drove the knife into the man's stomach, just below the rib cage. Fortunately for her, he was not wearing his jacket, or else it would have done little more than knock off one of his buttons. As it was, however, he was wearing only his white shirt. The knife penetrated the abdominal area and ended up puncturing his right lung. The man's expression changed immediately to one of total shock. The look in his eyes frightened Elaina. Trying to grab for her throat, he slowly began to sink to his knees. Red spots began to appear on his lip as he began to drown in his own blood. Elaina backed away in abject horror. He then fell on his face, driving the knife in further and leaving an ever-growing red spot on the carpet.

Day One, 7:00 a.m. (EST)—*AP news story—With futures down, the Dow is expected to open significantly lower this morning. Market analysts all agree that yesterday's assassination of President-elect Constanza has contributed greatly to the day's anticipated losses. His death has rekindled concerns that without Constanza's intervention in the Mexican legislature, the politicians inside the Mexican government will now renew their call to default on Mexico's debt to the United States in a show of hostility toward their northern neighbor. One analyst, under the condition of remaining anonymous, told this reporter that news of this possibility was not news in itself since it is understood by American banks that Mexico, and any other debtor nation for that matter, will never repay any money they owe to the U.S. government. He remarked cynically that that would be the responsibility of the U.S. taxpayer. He also said market concerns are such that if Mexico were to formally default on its debt, it might spur other third-world countries to follow suit. This action would then force the Federal Deposit Insurance Corporation, the governing body of all federally insured banks, to instruct many U.S. lenders to write off billions of dollars in foreign debt as being uncollectible, which would adversely affect their balance sheets and earnings and destroy the possibility of future dividend distributions to their stockholders for a considerable time.*

*   *   *

8:00 a.m. (EST)—It was turning out to be a beautiful day in the nation's capital. The dark clouds and the previous day's rain had disappeared during the evening, leaving only the fresh fragrance of wet vegetation behind.

Inside 1600 Pennsylvania Avenue, however, the situation was not so rosy, especially for one individual. Andrew Greenberg, chairman of the Federal Reserve's board of directors, was seated impatiently inside the Oval Office. His mood was one of anger and impatience, not panic, although the information he was bringing to the president would have sent virtually everyone else into a state of absolute dread. Instead, it was one of deep concern over the possible ramifications of the news once it was made public. He had made it known in no uncertain terms to the secretary to whom he had spoken that he had to speak to the president immediately. When told that the president was currently in a staff meeting and would not be available for at least another hour, he icily replied that if the president was not made available within five minutes, he would personally kick the door in upon the meeting and kick out everyone himself. Standing up to reveal his six-foot-six-inch, 250-pound frame in a menacing gesture, he apparently frightened the individual enough to ensure that he would follow through with his threat if his instructions were not immediately followed.

Greenberg sometimes disliked his position. Though prestigious in appearance, it often was a thankless task, like the holder for the extra point on a football team. Nobody noticed you unless you mishandled the snap from center. As long as the economy was purring along smoothly, inflation remained in check, and interest rates and unemployment stayed low, the politicians took the credit. But let recession creep into the equation or interest rates start to rise and the people on Capitol Hill would be screaming for hearings and demanding to know what you personally were going to do about it.

During his time with the Fed, Greenberg had more fully come to realize the enormous power wielded by his agency along with the tacit, although mostly unknown, trust the public placed in it. That's why he was extremely careful when he was in a public setting such as a luncheon or dinner party. A simple innocuous comment that the Fed was contemplating a bump in the prime rate could be overheard by an eager reporter, which would send Wall Street into a panic that would have reverberations not only in his country but around the world.

Because of this, Greenberg took his job seriously when it came to the dissemination of information from anyone in his office and why he had made the decision to deliver his information in person rather than trust its privacy to a telephone call.

Four-and-a-half minutes later, President James Collins came storming into the office with a look of extreme displeasure on his countenance. To double his anger was the fact that he knew Greenberg had total contempt for him and utter disdain for his presidency. Immediately behind him—like an obedient lapdog, thought Greenberg—strode the president's chief of staff, Anthony Rizzuto. Rizzuto's small, slightly humped shoulders coupled with his thick-rimmed glasses and large hook nose reminded Greenberg of a rat.

The animosity between him and Rizzuto, though not widely publicized, was well-known within the bureaucracy on Capitol Hill. The rift between them had stemmed from the White House's attempt, with fierce lobbying on Rizzuto's part, to get the Fed to lower interest rates prior to the last election campaign in an effort to improve Collins's shrinking poll numbers. The Fed chairman's refusal to succumb to the political pressure had been a major blow to the ego of the president's right-hand man, and though Collins had won re-election by a slim margin, it was a slap to Rizzuto's ego that he had never forgotten.

Greenberg turned his attention back to Collins. Except for the expensive suits, there was no similarity in their appearance. A full head taller, Collins could, in Greenberg's opinion, have been a poster boy for GQ magazine.

"What is so important that you had to drag me out of my staff meeting?" Collins demanded.

"Mr. President," Greenberg began, "something has happened early this morning in New York, and due to the sensitivity of the information I have, I believe it best that I speak to you in private."

"I think your secret will be safe with Anthony," Collins said.

"Mr. Rizzuto does not have the proper security clearance, Mr. President, and what I have to tell you is a matter of national security."

"I'll be the judge of that," Collins replied, getting more testy. "Anthony's security clearance is just a matter of formality."

Liar. He doesn't have the security clearance because he flunked the FBI's drug test. What you really want him around for is to protect you from sticking your foot in your mouth.

"As you wish. But I am on record as opposing your decision."

Collins raised his eyebrows in anger. He did not like being second-guessed. "I don't care for the direction this conversation is headed," he said. "Considering I supported your appointment as chairman, I think you would be more of a team player."

"Let's cut to the chase, Mr. President," replied Greenberg bluntly. "I wasn't your first choice for this position, nor your second for that matter. You don't like me any more than I like you. You wanted someone who would be your puppet when it came to formulating monetary policy. You simply read the tea leaves from members of your own party. They knew what their chances of survival would be if they went with your choice. It was politically expedient to do so."

""Now just a min—," Rizzuto began before being cut off by the Fed chairman.

"Oh, shut up, Anthony," Greenberg snapped, "and save it for someone who thinks you have something important to say. If you don't mind, Mr. President," he said, turning his attention back to the president, "I'll get directly to the reason why I'm here."

Stone silence.

"The economic survival of this country may be at stake," he began.

"What's that supposed to mean?" asked Collins, in a suddenly less-confrontational tone of voice. Despite his dislike for the Federal Reserve's chairman, he also knew Greenberg never issued idle threats.

"Let me give it to you in a nutshell," Greenberg began. "I have a private phone line which only the ten largest banks in New York have access to. Within a space of thirty minutes, I received phone calls this morning from seven of those banks. In the space of a few seconds, someone was able to gain access into every one of their computers. Virtually every checking account in every one of them, including their branches across the United States, was wiped out electronically and moved to locations unknown."

"So how much are we talking about?" Collins asked, seemingly unconcerned at this point.

"Combined, try approximately 3.5 trillion dollars," Greenberg replied evenhandedly.

Collins raised his eyebrows.

Silence ensued again before Rizzuto spoke up.

"I realize, Andrew," he began somewhat unconvincingly, "that it represents a lot of money, but I fail to see how a computer problem would affect the president or why this would fall into the category of national security."

Greenberg stiffened slightly, his blood pressure began to rise, and his blood began to boil. He looked up at Rizzuto with a slight sneer.

"You know, Anthony," he began slowly, "until now, I thought you might be ignorant on most things. But I was wrong. You're just plain stupid."

Collins rose up in anger. "Now just wait a minute!"

"No, Mr. President. YOU wait a minute!" Greenberg snapped, coming out of his chair in a menacing manner. "And you listen too, you little rodent," he added, looking directly into Rizzuto's eyes. "Seven of our largest banks have just been robbed of an amount exceeding our nation's budget, and it's not just the money in those banks that was taken. It's from their major corporate customers—the Exxons, Chevrons, IBM, Microsoft—all of them. In case it may have slipped your minds, we had a small problem with the banking and savings and loan industries back in the '80s, thanks largely to your party, Mr. President. That little debacle cost hundreds of billions. Compared to this, however, that will be chump change. Let me give you a best-case scenario. When, not if, word of this gets out on Wall Street, and believe me it will, there's going to be a panic that'll make the Great Depression look like a Sunday afternoon picnic. What are you going to tell investors? And how about all of those small individual depositors? Are you going to go on television and tell them how safe their money is after someone just pilfered all of their accounts out of what are supposedly the most secure banks around? They're going to want to make a beeline straight to those banks and start taking their money out of 'em so fast it'll make your heads spin—except there won't be any. It'll be just like 1929 all over. We won't be able to print new currency fast enough. And when the banks start running out of cash, there's going to be riots out in the streets. Interest rates will be back into double digits, and so will unemployment. I still have to figure out how the government is going to put money back into the banks before total panic sets in.

"I'm not even going to explain simple concepts like what the velocity of money means since I doubt either one of you two ever even took basic economics, or if you did, you probably flunked the course. In case you haven't noticed, the stock markets are already nervous and starting to take a beating, and you can bet it's going to get a lot worse before it gets better.

"And just what are you going to tell our allies and trading partners when our businesses stop buying goods from them? They're not going to be very happy. As far as the countries that don't like us, and there're lots of 'em, they'll be looking to retaliate any way they can. There's enough support in the Mexican government to approve formally defaulting on their debt to us. I wouldn't be surprised to find them debating that right now. And if they do, others will follow. That alone would be devastating to our banks. The only reason the markets haven't dropped any further is because they all know we'll never see a penny of it anyway. They're all having to borrow money from us to pay back the interest they owe us."

"So what are our options?" asked Collins, watching Greenberg head toward the door.

Greenberg turned around. "Options, Mr. President?" he asked with total askance in his voice. "You've got one option and one option only, sir." The word *sir* had a definite lack of respect in his voice. "You'd better sic some of those hatchet men you've been using on your political opponents to find out where all that money went to and get it back fast. I'll give it a week at the outside before the public finds out what has really happened. After that, what's left of this country won't be worth being president of. In case you two idiots don't understand the implications of this, I'll make it very simple. Someone has figured out how to hack into our banking system, which is just the same as waving a loaded gun in our faces. And there's one more thing. In addition to the FBI, you'd better get the CIA as well as Homeland Security involved."

"Why them?" Rizzuto asked, somewhat timidly.

Greenberg walked back over to the president's desk and slammed his copy of the newspaper onto it, jabbing his finger to the headline showing Constanza's assassination. "Because I don't believe in coincidences," he said. "Now if you don't mind, Mr. President, I've got some phone calls to make," storming out the room.

Chapter Three

9:00 a.m. (EST)—A meeting of the bank's executives was being convened at its downtown headquarters on Manhattan Island. There was no secretary present to take the minutes. The bank's CEO swore everyone in attendance to secrecy.

* * *

1:00 p.m. (Moscow time)—Elaina was in a state of extreme terror. Only a short time ago, she had killed a human being for the first time in her life, and even though she had not liked the general's adjutant, watching him slowly die as he fell in front of her had made her sick to her stomach to the point of vomiting. After she had thrown up in a waste basket near the bed, she knew she had to get out of the house quickly. The general would not only not take kindly to his assistant's death, but when he discovered the eavesdropping equipment in her possession and the bug she had planted in his study, she had no doubt as to her fate should she fall into his hands. Assessing her situation, Elaina had snuck out the back entrance of the house through the kitchen where she encountered the chef, telling him she wanted to take a stroll on the grounds of the dacha. She had guessed that she had maybe an hour or so before Kheraskov discovered the body, the fact that she was missing, and then institute a massive manhunt for her. She had not heard much before being found out herself, but enough to know that Kheraskov was planning something of enormous proportions.

Outside the house, she had quickly made her way past the main gate and on to the road leading toward Moscow, her planned destination. It had only taken a few minutes to get the attention of a passing small truck driver and hitch a ride with him. The ride into the city had taken twenty minutes. She had been forced to be as pleasant as possible to her benefactor, who was only too willing to carry on a conversation with such a beautiful passenger. He had dropped her off near Gorky Park where she needed to accomplish the first of her two tasks in her escape plans. Sitting down on a specific vacant park bench, Elaina opened her small purse and pulled out the same pen and paper she had used earlier to listen into Kheraskov's meeting. She thought for a moment before composing her small message and then folding the paper in a certain way. Finishing, she glanced in every direction to make sure she was unobserved. She stood up, leaned down, picked up the leg of the bench, laid the paper underneath it and set the leg back down on it. She then nonchalantly sat down again and pretended to take in the scenery, briefly glancing at her watch. Deciding she had remained long enough, Elaina stood up and walked away.

There will always be someone watching this bench between 7:00 a.m. and 5:00 p.m. who will know what to do if a message is left under this bench. Make sure you remain on the bench for at least ten minutes. After that, simply go to where you need to.

Elaina could not know that her actions had been observed from the moment she had sat on the bench, nor what had happened afterward. At about four o'clock that afternoon, another individual walked in an unsteady manner up to the same park bench and sat on it, a man in his midthirties who was obviously drunk to the untrained eye. In one hand he carried something in a small paper bag, which he pretended to hide from any passersby. Occasionally, he would lift the paper bag to his lips, indicating there was a bottle inside. In his other hand, he held a sandwich that he sometimes took a bite from. Leaning back, he seemed to take on the appearance of a typical vagrant who most of the park's sightseers did their best to avoid, which was exactly what the young man wanted. He staggered to stand up, and then in an almost imperceptible move, he bent over, lifted the leg of the bench up, removed the tiny slip of paper, and lurched to an upright position. He then staggered off in the same direction he had come from, one of the many vagrants who occupied the park.

His walk eventually took him to the Moscow subway. Paying the small fare, he took a free newspaper off one of the newsstands and boarded one of the trains, folding the newspaper in the shape of a funnel after stepping on to the subway car. Glancing up and down the rows of passengers, he spotted his intended target, an elderly man wearing a gray baseball cap. He then placed the small piece of paper he had received inside the folded newspaper and began walking forward. Any sense of drunkenness would have totally disappeared although the swaying of the subway still gave the illusion of uncertainty of anyone moving about. As he passed the man in the baseball cap, the man paused and slightly tipped the front of the newspaper upward with the skill of hours of practice. The piece of paper rolled backward through the newspaper and fell into the lap of his intended target. "Two!" He smiled to himself.

*   *   *

Kheraskov stood over the lifeless body of his adjutant along with two other of his subordinates.

"She must have something to hide in order to do this," he said grimly. "Find her."

He noticed something on the floor and went over to examine it. It turned out to be a small length of wiring attached to a headpiece.

"Check the entire house for bugs, especially my study," he added. "Plus, call all of our stations in Europe and have them keep their eyes on the American embassies. That is the only place she can feel safe."

*   *   *

2:30 p.m. (Moscow time)—Elaina's next destination was a small liquor shop located perhaps half a mile away. She walked into the establishment where a number of customers were examining potential purchases and spotted a woman unpacking a box containing bottles of liquor.

She stood behind the woman and asked, "Do you have any Stolichnaya vodka?"

She spotted a slight flinch in the woman's shoulders although she did not turn around. "I don't believe we carry that brand," she replied.

"I'm sure I heard your son say that you did," Elaina said. "Perhaps if we went to the back of the shop and ask him."

The woman stood up and smiled. "Let's go and see, shall we?" she said.

The woman led Elaina through a door behind the cash register where she found herself in a room filled with shelves that contained a voluminous number of unopened boxes.

"Stay here. I will be back for you after the shop closes" were the only words she spoke. She then turned around and walked back into the front of the shop.

The minutes dragged and seemed like hours to Elaina. Her mind let her imagination roam and made her think of what Kheraskov would do to her if he caught her. The man who had recruited her had warned her that no one ever came out through his interrogation methods alive. He had given her a capsule to swallow if the need arose, but even though the thought repulsed her from what it represented, he had convinced her that it was far less painful and much quicker than the alternative. She kept it in a false bottom of her lipstick.

*   *   *

8:00 p.m. (Moscow time)—The transit bus halted on a lonely dirt road intersection twenty miles outside Moscow as nighttime settled in, and a sole occupant wearing a gray baseball cap shuffled off. After the bus left, the man waited for the dust to settle before crossing the road. He walked about a quarter of a mile down the road in relative darkness and, making sure he was unobserved, located a specific landmark among some bushes and made his way toward it. Glancing at his watch, he determined he had twenty-five minutes to complete his task. Rummaging among the bushes, he pulled out a small metal box and set it in a relatively open area. He extended an antenna that rose about three feet above the box and pressed a button to activate the powerful transmitter. The last step in the sequence was to open the top of the box which revealed a keyboard. He then pulled out the small sheet of paper that had been passed to him on the subway and began entering the information into the miniature computer. Verifying he had made no mistakes, he hit ENTER, and in a matter of nanoseconds, the information was transmitted to a satellite in geosynchronous orbit two hundred miles above the earth and forwarded to its final destination.

As quickly as he had set up the transmitter, he dismantled it and returned it to its original state. The man knew it was highly unlikely that two receivers of the KGB would have picked up the signal at the same time in order to triangulate and locate its source, but he was unwilling to risk detection. His watch revealed he had over fifteen minutes to return to the spot where the bus had let him off, plenty of time to walk the distance. After he had reached the spot, he waited patiently until he could hear an approaching car emit two brief honks. Stepping out into the open, he made himself visible to the car. It stopped briefly in order to allow the man to open the passenger door and get in.

"I had to honk, you know," the driver commented somewhat dryly. "I thought I saw something moving on the road." Both men smiled as the car then continued on its course back to Moscow.

* * *

8:30 a.m. (EST)—Across the Potomac River in Langley, Virginia, a less confrontational situation from what had occurred between Greenberg and Collins was about to take place. Robert Mills, newly appointed director of the Central Intelligence Agency was just entering CIA headquarters when a young man walked up to him.

"I have a FLASH message for you, sir," he said.

"What is it?" Mills asked.

"It's encrypted, for your eyes only," the man replied.

Mills frowned. This was not how he had anticipated his morning would start. He headed straight to the elevator that would take him to his office. Opening the outside door, he found Jenny busily pounding away at the computer in front of her. She paused briefly to greet him then returned to her work. Mills returned her smile then headed toward the door that led to his private office. Closing the door behind him, he opened the folded sheet of paper he had been given to examine it. Inside were four encoded words. Mills frowned again. It was his experience that the shorter the message, the more ominous. The message, he knew, would be doubly encrypted with the first word identifying the source of the person who sent the message without revealing the identity of the person himself. It would tell him what file to go to in the basement downstairs to unscramble the remaining words. The basement referred to was a place not many outside the CIA knew existed. The term "acceptable risk" did not apply when it came to its protection. Inside the thick vault contained a series of filing cabinets, and inside those cabinets included the information on every mole currently under the management of the CIA. There were not as many files now as there had once been. Under the Carter administration, there had been a concerted effort to gut the intelligence-gathering efforts of the country, and only with the Reagan administration's hard work had there been an effort to rebuild it. Even so, the files were only half as full as they had once been since the ability to employ new recruits were hampered by the simple fact that people were less willing to put their lives at risk for someone they perceived to be untrustworthy in protecting their identity.

Mills got up from his desk and headed back out the door. He did not write down the file number but committed it to memory as he told Jenny he would be back in about thirty minutes. Inside the elevator he took out his keys, inserted one into a lock, and turned it, allowing him access to the basement. As he stepped outside the elevator, the atmosphere seemed to change immediately. A man in a dark blue business suit was waiting for him as he stepped off. From this moment on, Mills knew that his every move would be scrutinized by unseen eyes above until he entered the secret vault at the end of the hall. Both men walked silently down the short corridor, and Mills entered a five-digit code into the keyboard on the wall. He then stepped aside to allow his companion to do the same. Once the correct code had been entered, the door automatically opened on silent hinges and the two men stepped inside.

The room they entered was no bigger than a large closet. It contained one small chair and a monitor built into the wall in front of it and a heavy metal door to the screen's left. Mills sat in the chair, pressed a red button next to the screen, and waited. A metallic voice asked him a series of questions to which he responded. A small flash occurred that the computer used to conduct a retinal scan. Once complete, the metal door began to slowly open, allowing Mills and the man with him to walk into one of the most secret rooms in the country. It was spacious with a series of filing cabinets lining its walls. Mills recalled the letters of the FLASH message and located the correct filing cabinet. Opening the second drawer, he located the file he wanted. It was almost empty, indicating the mole writing the message was either a recent recruit or, up until now, had had nothing to report. Mills laid the mole's code on top of the cabinet and then proceeded to convert the words into English. They were *Kheraskov, Constanza,* and *Banks.* After the last word was a question mark.

Day Two—*API midday news report—News of revised earnings has sent major tremors throughout the banking industry. Shock waves have quickly reached investors on Wall Street, and the Dow has dropped sharply early in the day's trading session. Unconfirmed reports with the Federal Deposit Insurance Corporation indicate that regulators will be conducting extensive credit investigations on at least one bank in New York. There is a strong possibility that some of the large money-center banks may be asked to write off billions of dollars of nonperforming foreign debt. This comes on the heels of recent rumors that the U.S.'s largest debtor, Mexico, is considering a formal default of its debt in protest of the way the U.S. is dealing with the immigration issue. The announcement has again raised the issue that banks will have to alter their credit policies in the future, making it even more expensive for corporations to borrow money. Analysts believe that this tightening would have the greatest impact in the real estate markets of New England, Florida, and Arizona.*

*   *   *

11:30 a.m. (EST)—Robert Mills sat alone in the CIA's cafeteria, munching thoughtfully on a cold roast beef sandwich and potato chips while trying to ponder the meaning of the three words he had earlier deciphered. Kheraskov, he knew all about as the hard-line communist in charge of the KGB. Obviously, Constanza was self-explanatory, but he was stumped as to the meaning of banks.

He looked up to see the same man who had brought him the FLASH message. Accompanying him was a very tall man, and although he had never met him personally, he knew him all too well by reputation. *I suppose I'm about to find out.*

*   *   *

8:00 a.m. (CST)—During his leisurely walk down the open hallway of the huge atrium of the building on the Southwest Freeway in Houston, Texas, Doug Warner gave a friendly wave or said hello to his fellow FDIC employees. Doug was feeling much refreshed, having just completed a two-week vacation with his wife Jamie that had taken them through most of Western Europe. Now it was Jonathan's turn, and he was glad to return his best friend's favor for holding down the fort in his absence. As he reached the door that led into the set of offices belonging to the Investigations Unit and was turning the knob, a woman's scream reached his ears. Doug smiled and opened the door, having a good idea as to the source. The first sight to greet his eyes was a large desk, and behind it sat an elderly lady with a scowl on her face. Sally Virgil looked none too happy.

"Where is he?" she yelled.

"Who are you talking about?" Doug asked, not too convincingly.

"You know perfectly well who," she snapped at him. "Where is Jonathan Walker? I know he's got to be somewhere in this building because you're here. I know he did it."

Jonathan and Doug always carpooled into work.

"Oh, him," Doug answered. "He decided to stop off at MacDonald's across the street and grab something to eat. What did he supposedly do?"

"This!" she retorted angrily, flinging an object at him. It turned out to be a rubber snake.

"You just missed hitting me in the face by that much," he said in his best Don Adams imitation from the '60s sitcom *Get Smart*. Ah, the old rubber-snake-hidden-in-the-secretary's-desk trick.

"The only reason I know it wasn't you is because you didn't get in until late last night," Sally said in a frustrated voice. "Why do you two keep doing this to me? I just lost ten years of my life, and I don't have that many left."

"Oh, Sally," Doug grinned. "We only do it because we love you so much."

Just then, the door opened behind Doug, and Jonathan Walker walked in. In his right hand was a small vase filled with flowers.

Doug turned as Jonathan strode up next to him.

"I'd tread lightly if I were you," he said in a low voice.

"Here's something for the world's best secretary," said Jonathan in a lighthearted tone.

"Don't you dare try to butter me up with those," Sally said stone-faced. "It's going to take a lot more than that to placate me."

"Gosh, Doug," said Jonathan thoughtfully, "do you think a lunch at Olive Garden might help any?"

"I'm not sure," replied Doug, putting his curled hand to his chin in an expression of thoughtfulness. "That may be a thought."

"Oh, you two," Sally fumed, picking up her stapler and pretending she was going to throw it at them. "Get out of here before I report you to Mark."

Mark Duncan was the officer-in-charge of the Investigations Department.

Doug and Jonathan grinned, dutifully turned to their left in a display of contrition and scurried off.

"Buy you a cup of coffee?" Jonathan asked his best friend of nearly thirty years.

"Deal," replied Doug.

"I want to hear everything about your trip," said Jonathan. "It'll be a good way to get warmed up for mine."

Doug grinned as they walked over to the coffee bar.

"Everything was perfect," he began. "Every hotel, every restaurant, every sight—you just couldn't ask for anything better. Jamie's heart just about melted when I took her on that gondola ride in Venice. She was in romantic nirvana. I can truly say that there are marks on the tarmac at Heathrow where I had to drag her back on to the plane to come home."

"Just don't mention anything to Mary about the gondola ride until we get back from our vacation," Jonathan laughed. "She might insist on me changing our itinerary."

"I don't think you have much to worry about," said Doug. "When you guys are cruising on those still waters along the Alaskan coast, she's going to have too many other things on her mind."

As they were carrying on their lighthearted conversation and fixing their coffee, Sally walked up to them.

"Listen, Sally," Jonathan began, "You know I didn't mean to—"

"Never mind about that," returned Sally seriously with a wave of her hand. "Mark wants to see you two immediately, and he doesn't look very happy."

"Now what have we done to him?" Jonathan asked, puzzled.

"I can't think of anything—lately," replied Doug, grinning.

"I don't think it's you two he's upset with," Sally said. "He just got off the phone with some people in DC. Whatever it was, it can't be good news."

Doug and Jonathan looked at each other with puzzled expressions but picked up their coffee and headed to their boss's office. "What does Washington want with us mortals?" Jonathan wondered out loud.

Jonathan and Doug had known Mark ever since they had been hired by the FDIC six years ago. They both had an immense amount of respect for their supervisor. He demanded a lot from everyone under him, but he also wanted them to have fun. He was always arranging activities away from the office that he encouraged everyone to attend: bowling, putt-putt golf, and an occasional backyard barbecue among them. As a result of his efforts, the Investigations Department was the most productive unit within the FDIC. His philosophy was very simple—he demanded a lot from his people, but he also made sure that good work was rewarded.

Mark's two biggest stars were Doug Warner and Jonathan Walker. Their impact had been felt within days of their arrival at the FDIC when they had been assigned the responsibility of collecting on "specialized" assets owned by the FDIC—litigation, judgments, and bankruptcies that had come under its control when a bank had collapsed. The first thing the legal department had learned about them was their tenacity and determinedness to bring any perpetrators of criminal activity to justice in the court system and that their efforts knew no boundaries. Mark attributed their doggedness to their prior experience of having been dismissed from their previous employer, a medium-sized bank in the southwest Houston area.

Mark had been only partially correct in his assessment of the two. In fact, most of their determination had come years earlier during the four years they had spent in Texas A&M's corps of cadets as roommates. Jonathan and Doug had developed a closeness that they had developed while undergoing the rigors of military training and learned the value of camaraderie, especially during their freshman year as members of A&M's national champion precision fish drill team and then their junior year when they had tried out and earned places as members of the Ross Volunteers, the elite members of the corps who also comprised the honor guard for the governor of Texas. Jonathan learned that Doug's parents had fled East Germany in the mid-1960s while Doug was only ten. They had managed to escape just before Russia had closed the border and built the Berlin wall. Jonathan developed a great respect for Doug's parents in learning of the rigors they had been forced to undertake in fleeing the communists and the sacrifices they had made for their son in getting him immersed in the American school system.

Doug had worked diligently to obtain a scholarship into Texas A&M's corps of cadets. He and Jonathan had taken the definition of an Aggie to heart. It was a definition that Jonathan had had engraved on a wooden plaque and hung on the wall above his desk. It read, "An Aggie does not lie, cheat, or steal, nor does he tolerate others who do."

Because of their zeal in the aggressive way they performed their duties, Jonathan and Doug had earned nicknames from the legal department located a few floors above them, Rambo and Robocop. The first hint had come in the second week of their employment when Jonathan had been called to testify in a jury trial as the FDIC's expert witness against the accountant of a bank who had embezzled over two million dollars from his employer. During his cross-examination, the opposing attorney had attempted to blame Jonathan of falsely accusing his client, which turned out to be a huge mistake. In a very icy tone of voice, Jonathan looked at the jury and began to explain very succinctly how the defendant had defrauded the bank by cooking the books to his advantage, and when the attorney tried to cut him off, Jonathan stood up in the witness chair and told him to shut up until he had finished answering the question he had been given. A verbal tirade had ensued between the two with Jonathan having to be restrained by the judge and ordered to sit down. All the while, the FDIC's attorney had sat quietly in his chair, doing everything he could to maintain his mirth over the way Jonathan had acquitted himself. When he had returned to the office, the first thing he had done was to tell his colleagues what had transpired. They had each made it a point to attend future trials and witness fireworks between the opposing counsel and Jonathan or Doug.

When the two had entered Mark's office, he got up from his desk and walked over to shut the door behind them. He then sat down on the front of his desk and looked grimly at them.

"Okay, you two," he began. "Here's the bottom line, and it's going to affect you, Jonathan, more than Doug. As of this moment, Jonathan, your vacation's put on the back burner, and both of you are flying out first thing tomorrow morning to New York."

Jonathan and Doug looked at each other. "Now what is so important up there that it's got to drag me away from my trip?" Jonathan demanded angrily. "Mary and I have been planning this vacation for months, and you approved it!"

Mark understood the nature of Jonathan's anger, which is why he did not raise his own voice.

"I know, I know, Jonathan," he tried to explain as calmly as he could. "I've been arguing with DC about it for the last fifteen minutes. I told them that you had other plans scheduled, but they wouldn't listen. They picked you two specifically and wouldn't budge."

"Why us?" asked Doug. "Why not somebody else?"

"Because, evidently, word has managed to circulate up all the way up there about your exploits down here," Mark replied, shrugging his shoulders. "They said 'Hey, we need your two best people to do some quiet investigating over some files'—and that's you two. They said they don't want any more than two because they want this to be a low profile on whatever's going on, and a bunch of people running around up there would be making too many people ask too many questions. Have you two been reading the *Chronicle* lately? Evidently, whatever's going on is causing somebody to sweat bullets. They're sending down your tickets by Fed Ex right now, and they'll be delivered here this afternoon. And whatever you uncover up there, you are only to communicate it to me."

Jonathan got up with an angry look across his face and stormed out of the office, leaving Doug and Mark to look at each other.

"If I didn't know him any better than I do," Doug said, "I'd lay you even money that he'd be typing his resignation this minute. He and Mary need this vacation."

"Don't you think I know that?" Mark replied, exasperated. "I did everything I could think of to get you guys out of this, but Washington wouldn't listen. It was like talking to a brick wall."

Doug had known Mark long enough to know that he was being sincere in his apology. Both of them had known about the strain that had been developing in the relationship between Jonathan and Mary for some time.

Not that they still didn't love each other. Jonathan had loved Mary almost from the first time he had spotted her over in Dublin, Ireland. He had gone there on vacation while stationed at Lakenheath, England, as a navigator in an F-15E Eagle of the Forty-eighth Tactical Fighter Wing in the USAF. Up until then, his only love had been in sitting in the backseat of his aircraft doing mach-two-plus, low-level passes over simulated targets and then pulling up in a vertical climb to an altitude of sixty-five thousand feet in a matter of just seconds.

Using a three-day pass, he had decided to take the opportunity to observe his temporary home and wander across the widest part of England. He soon found himself in Holyhead and looking across the Irish Sea, which separated the two countries by a mere seventy miles. On a whim, he had taken the short trip across to the Irish coast in order to take in the atmosphere of Dublin. Stepping into a small curio shop while wandering the cobblestone streets in Dublin, he had discovered her behind the counter of an antiquated cash register. Mary had looked up as a matter of habit when the ring of the small bell attached to the door announced the arrival of a new customer. When his eyes had met hers, he had become infatuated. Not only had he been taken in by her green eyes, but also with the soft shoulder-length curls of her amber hair and her distinct accent, which had caused him to be totally smitten.

Jonathan had immediately asked for an extended leave of absence from his duties and had begun visiting the shop on a daily basis until he had worked up the courage to ask her out on a date. She had, in turn, found his insecurity over the unfamiliar surroundings of a different culture to be both quaint and amusing. Over the next several months, he had taken the train ride across the English countryside virtually every free weekend where he had spent every Sunday morning alongside her in church. Finally, he found the nerve to ask for permission from her dad for her hand in marriage. Having been given his consent, he then—that evening on a date to a local pub and in front of a lively crowd—had knelt before her, posed the question, and pulled out a small box from his shirt pocket. She had clasped her hands over her mouth in total disbelief and, unable to speak, bobbed her head frantically in the affirmative. When her grinning parents had emerged from a concealed place in the establishment, her joy knew no bounds and she leaped into his arms and covered his face with kisses. Jonathan immediately bought a round of drinks for everyone in the pub. From that moment on, however, things had been a blur for him. Mary had immediately taken over control of all the wedding plans, and the only task he had been requested to do was to choose his best man—Doug, who had only been too glad to fly over with his wife to attend the ceremony. Both Doug and Jamie had given their hearty approval to Jonathan's choice, and Mary had been equally in favor of Jonathan's friends.

After the wedding, with Doug and Jamie preparing to fly back, Mary had promised Jamie to write often as she was eager to learn all about the storied land Jonathan called home (Texas) and whether or not everyone there owned an oil rig or traveled by horseback and rounded up cattle. Laughing, Jamie had promised Jonathan that she would do her best to let Mary down easy.

*   *   *

7:00 p.m. (CST)—Jonathan sat across the kitchen table from Mary that evening with his hands folded.

"I'll quit tomorrow if you want me to," he said despondently. "Just say the word, and we can still go on our vacation."

"And then what will you do?" she answered, totally frustrated. "You've worked alongside Doug ever since you left the air force. He helped you get your first job when you got back here. The vacation might be good for a while, but how are you going to feel when we get back? You'll be miserable, and so will I."

"So what do you want me to do?" he asked.

"Go on your trip to New York," she said. "You said Mark will have the FDIC reimburse us for all of our nonrefundable costs. If that's the case, I'll start rescheduling our trip for when you get back. I'd just like to throttle him for doing this."

"It wasn't him," Jonathan told her. "It was those idiots in their Washington palaces that made the decision."

Mary stood up resignedly. "Why do you have to be so good at what you do?" she asked with a sign of defeat in her voice. "I'll go upstairs and get your suitcase ready."

Chapter Four

Day Three—Jonathan awoke at four o'clock the following morning, showered, and quickly got dressed. Mary, who had risen at the same time, was downstairs fixing both of them breakfast. Their two daughters, Sandra and Debbie, were scheduled to arrive home from their college studies later on in the afternoon. Initially, the girls were supposed to watch the house while their parents were away on vacation. As it was, Mary would be happy to have their company while Jonathan was away. The meal was eaten in relative silence with Jonathan promising to call her that evening with a telephone number where he and Doug could be reached.

Precisely at five, Doug pulled in front of the Walker driveway and honked his horn. Jonathan and Mary walked together with Mary still in her bathrobe. Jonathan tossed his suitcase into the backseat of the car while she dutifully opened the passenger-side door to allow him to climb in. Closing it and leaning through the rolled-down window, she said, "You two watch out for each other. Jamie and I will do the same here." Standing away from the car, she waved as it drove off.

Since Jonathan was not in a talkative mood, the ride to Houston's Intercontinental Airport was accomplished in relative silence. Doug parked in one of the remote parking lots where the two removed their suitcases and boarded a shuttle bus that would take them to their desired terminal. Once inside, they walked up to a check-in counter, and since it was not yet 6:00 a.m., they were able to get checked in to their flight almost immediately. As they walked to their departure gate, Doug stopped momentarily to examine the headlines of the *Houston Chronicle* and let out a low whistle as he read the main news story: "Constanza Assassination Causes Major Bank Upheaval in New York."

"Do you think this might be why we're heading up there?" he asked his friend.

"I wouldn't be surprised," nodded Jonathan. "I suppose we'll know for sure in about three or four hours."

UPI midday—"*For only the second day in its history, the Dow Jones suspended trading when the market fell over six hundred points in less than three hours. The automatic trigger to halt trading was done in hopes that nervous traders will have their fears eased before trading resumes tomorrow.*"

* * *

Mary sat across the desk from Pastor Hart. Her eyes were red from tears although she had managed to stop crying.

"You know he loves you, Mary," he said. "But we also both know he has a few issues that he's still having to work through concerning his parents. And he will."

"But why do all of these roadblocks keep happening to us?" she asked, totally discouraged. "Why does God do this?"

"I don't necessarily believe God is actually the direct cause of your problems," he replied. "I think that it's Satan, who would like nothing better than to destroy your marriage, and he's probably got his hands in this. But you know, God will never give us anything we cannot handle. And your faith is strong, Mary. So is Jonathan's. Now don't worry about the work here. You know that I've already made arrangements for some of the ladies from your group to pick up the slack while you're gone. Take as much time as you need. And we'll make sure you're on the prayer list effective immediately."

"Thank you, Pastor Hart."

* * *

Richard Black, chairman of the bank's board of directors, called the impromptu meeting to order as he passed out a single sheet of paper to the men seated around the table.

"As you can all see," he began, "the comptroller has changed the rules of the game somewhat. Ever since the *American Banker* hit the newsstands this morning, my office has been flooded with dozens of phone calls from our customers. They are all asking the same question. They want to know if their money is safe."

"Can they do this, Dick? I mean, is it legal?" asked one of the men.

"The answer to both questions is yes," Black said. "And what's worse, our legal people tell me that they can basically do whatever they want."

An angrier voice spoke up. "So we've got a bunch of yahoos down in Washington telling us that because of some accounting gimmick, we've got to revise our earnings to show a loss of over $300 million for the quarter. That's going to make the stockholders real happy."

"I'm afraid the bad news doesn't end there," Black continued. "We're about to get a visit from the comptroller's office."

"I'll tell you what this is all about," said the angry voice. "It's that guy Miller. He's that Harvard hotshot kid who just got himself appointed to run the FDIC. What he's aiming for is a spot on Collins's cabinet, and he doesn't care who he has to step on to get there."

Just then, the door to the conference room opened, and a woman walked in, bearing a rolled-up newspaper in her hand. She handed it to Black and walked out of the room. The chairman flipped through the paper until he came to the business section and pulled it out. He glanced at the headlines briefly before tossing it on to the table in front of him.

"Just what I was afraid of," he said.

Those nearest to the paper glanced at it. Dan Berry, the one possessing the angry voice, picked it up and began reading out loud.

"News of the revised earnings ordered by the comptroller's office has sent major shock waves throughout the banking industry. The Dow Jones had fallen over four hundred points in early trading, and reports from an unnamed source within the FDIC indicate that regulators are now conducting extensive credit examinations into at least one large bank. There is a strong possibility that banks will be instructed to write off billions of foreign debt as either nonperforming or uncollectible. This news comes on the heels that at least one debtor nation is considering making a formal default of its debt to the United States. This announcement has raised the issue of the concern that banks will be forced to tighten their credit policies in the future, making it more expensive for corporations to borrow money. There are fears among many noted analysts that the prime interest rate may soon rise to double digits, something this country has not witnessed since the late 1970s under the Carter administration. Most analysts believe this would most adversely affect the retirement sections of the United States such as Florida, Texas, and Arizona."

"I believe we can safely assume which country the article is referring to," said Black, "and the bank being examined probably means us since we're Mexico's biggest lender."

"Good grief, Dick!" snapped Berry. "You're talking like we're trying to figure out what to order for lunch! Don't you people have any idea what the implications of this are? If the Feds tell us we're going to write off all of our nonperforming foreign debt, then we're technically bankrupt."

"Take it easy, Dan," said Black. "Let's not go off the deep end. Let's hear what they have to say first. Miller's not all that bad."

A knock on the door preceded the secretary entering again.

"Excuse me, Mr. Black," she said. "A Mr. Miller is here to see you."

"Tell him I'll be right out," he answered.

"So he has the nerve to show up himself," snarled Berry.

He got up from his chair and left the room. Moments later, he came back with two men at his heels.

"Gentlemen, I believe you all know Mr. Henry Miller. The man with him is Mr. Greg Watts. He's also with the FDIC."

Miller carried himself well. He appeared to be in his mid-thirties and had the look of a man who worked out regularly.

"Gentlemen, he began. I won't waste any of your time."

He sat his briefcase on the table, opened it, and passed out several copies of a document around to the various members seated. Across the top of the first page were written in large bold letters:

"NOTICE OF DETERMINATION"

The last page of the document had the signature and seal of the comptroller of the currency. Miller gave them a few moments to study the document before speaking.

"I would like to call your attention to the second page of the notice where it talks about the requirement to abate determination. After our examination is complete, you will be given six months to clear up the deficiencies in the report. Your biggest obstacle, I'm sure, will be in raising the funds required to meet your minimal capital needs. If you fail to present us with an adequate demonstration that you are solving the problem, then the comptroller's office will appoint the FDIC as receiver. If a healthy bank cannot be found to step in, the FDIC will then take over and pay off the insured depositors. Does anyone have any questions?"

"Yeah, I've got a couple," Sam Berry's voice cut in with unmistakable venom. "I'd like to know just who gives you the right to start changing the rules on us. We've been told for years to lend money to a bunch of two-bit third-world countries, including Mexico, even though none of them would ever meet our minimal standards. Then you tell us you won't count the bad loans against us. You're stabbing us in the back with this little stunt."

"First of all, Mr. Berry, I know what most of you think about me. I am completely on your side in this matter, and I don't like this situation any more than you do. And all I can tell you is that this came down from way up top. I can only assure you that I had nothing personally with this decision."

"That means it came from Collins. His approval ratings are in the toilet, and he's hoping to show everyone how tough he's ready to get, isn't he? He's proven that he's a Marxist, and now that everyone's realized it, it's too late to do anything about it."

"I'm afraid it's a little more complicated than that, and I won't get into a political debate about the president," Miller admitted. "But don't ask because I can't get into any specifics."

Berry stared at him before finally speaking. "Oh my God! It's more than just this bank, isn't it? If that's the case, what happened to us was no computer glitch. Someone has figured out a way to hack into our systems, haven't they?"

Miller remained silent and stone-faced, which spoke volumes.

Chapter Five

The jet landed safely at Kennedy, but since neither Doug nor Jonathan felt any great rush to get to their targeted destination, they decided to have their taxi driver take them to their hotel where they unloaded their suitcases. They then took another cab to the bank. On their way, they found their cab driver was in a talkative mood.

"Have you guys heard about what's happened on Wall Street? They just shut it down just a while ago. They say one of the big banks is in big trouble. I'm sure glad I don't have anything in it right now."

Doug and Jonathan looked at each other with consternation on their faces. They arrived at an enormous building where their instructions told them to go to the sixteenth floor and ask to speak to a Mrs. Hawthorn.

"Are you ready for this?" Doug asked Jonathan as they began their ascent in the elevator.

"Let's get this over with, as soon as we find out what the heck we're supposed to do," answered his friend. "I've got more important things on my mind."

As the door opened to reveal the floor housing all the bank's executives, Jonathan turned to Doug and remarked in a low voice, "So this is how the other half lives."

They stepped on to the deep plush carpeting, and Doug walked up to what was obviously the receptionist's desk and spoke to the attractive young lady sitting behind it. Smiling, she asked, "May I help you?"

"Yes ma'am, you may," he replied. "My name is Doug Warner, and this is Jonathan Walker. We're with the FDIC office in Houston, and we're here to see Mrs. Hawthorn."

When Doug mentioned the FDIC, the woman's countenance changed immediately.

"If you'll have a seat, I'll go get her," she replied, stone-faced. She walked off down the long corridor.

As they turned around to sit on a nearby couch, Doug whispered to Jonathan, "What did I say?"

"I don't know," Jonathan answered. "But you would think that you just slapped her mother or something."

Five minutes later, the young lady returned, accompanied by a much older woman who did her best to put on a pleasant appearance. "Mr. Warner, Mr. Walker," she said, "if you'll follow me, we'll get you set up in one of our conference rooms. The files you are supposed to be looking at are already there." Leading them to a wooden door, she opened it to reveal a large office with a big rectangular table surrounded by a dozen or so executive chairs.

"Over there we have a coffee bar with all the fixings, and over here is the refrigerator. Inside of it, you'll find fruit juices and some cookies. Just help yourself. The company restaurant is located on the third floor. Do you need anything before I take off?"

"I don't think so right now," Doug replied. "Thank you for your help, and we'll let you know if we need anything."

"Well, if I can get you anything, my desk is the second on the left when you walk out the door." She turned around and walked out, leaving them to their own devices.

Jonathan turned to Doug. "Let's get on with it," he said, walking over to an empty seat.

*   *   *

At about five o'clock in the evening, Elaina could hear the sounds of the woman closing up the shop, the last being that of a metal shade being brought down over the entrance. Moments later, she joined Elaina in the back room. "Follow me," she said simply, leading her young charge to a set of well-worn stairs at the back of the room. The woman, whose name remained unknown to Elaina, led her up the stairs to a tiny, sparsely furnished apartment consisting of a combined living room area with a kitchen stuck in the corner and a bedroom barely large enough to squeeze a single bed and a dresser into. The woman turned on a light switch, and a single bulb in the living room area came on. So this is how my countrymen are forced to live, Elaina thought.

The woman turned and looked at Elaina. "You are very beautiful," she said. "Under different circumstances, I might like to hear what brought you to my shop, but that will not be possible right now. You do not know my name, and I do not wish to know yours. A delivery truck will come tonight to bring me a shipment for my store. When the driver arrives, he will unload some boxes and then get back into his truck and wait for five minutes. That will allow you enough time to get into the back. There is a small secret compartment hidden in the flooring, which is where you will be concealed. It is not big, but since you are not either, it will not be too cramped. There will be enough food and water in the compartment to last the entire journey. Do not speak unless you are spoken to by him, and do exactly what he tells you to do."

"Where is he taking me?" Elaina asked her benefactor.

"I do not know." The woman shrugged her shoulders. "Nor do I wish to. The less each of us knows, the better, should one of us be found out. Are you hungry?"

"A little," Elaina replied. In truth, she was quite famished, having not eaten since supper the previous evening.

The woman nodded and went into the kitchen area, opened the small refrigerator, and pulled out a covered pot. She then set it on the nearby stove and began warming up its contents. Elaina sat down on the couch and tried unsuccessfully to relax. After a few minutes, the aroma of what appeared to be some sort of stew began to permeate the living quarters. The woman then invited Elaina to come over to a table where she brought out some fresh-baked bread and some butter. Elaina was on her second slice when a steaming bowl was set before her. Elaina thought she had probably tasted better before, but she could not remember when. Her hostess did not seem overly concerned at the way her young charge attacked her meal, nor did she act surprised when a second helping was requested. In due course, however, the meal was finally disposed of, and the dishes were washed and put away.

The woman turned to Elaina once again. "The journey will be strenuous," she said, "but it will be as safe as they can possibly make it. Just remember to follow every instruction to the letter. There must be no deviations. Do you understand?"

"Yes."

"Very well. Your ride will be here in about two hours. Why don't you lie down and try to sleep until then."

Elaina was grateful for the opportunity to close her eyes and escape from the stress of the day, even if only for a short period of time. She went into the bedroom and lay down, falling asleep almost immediately.

*   *   *

9:00 p.m. (Moscow time)—Elaina awoke with a start to a gentle shaking from the woman.

"Your transportation is here," she said. "Quickly. You must waste no time."

Elaina got out of bed and followed the woman downstairs to the back of the shop. A truck had backed up and was parked close to the building's open door with the engine still running, and she could vaguely see the outline of an individual behind the wheel but was unable to make out any of his features. Elaina climbed aboard first, followed by the woman who bent over and lifted up a flap hidden into the flooring.

"Lie on your back, and after I close the door, lock it."

Elaina looked at her benefactor. Impulsively, she hugged the woman. "Thank you for everything," she said. She then climbed into the cramped space, got as comfortable as she could, and lay on her back so that she was looking up. "Good luck," said the woman, smiling.

Elaina returned the smile as the door was lowered. Darkness encompassed her except for tiny slivers of light showing through the cracks in the flooring. She could hear the woman's footsteps fading in the distance. Thirty seconds later, she felt the truck begin to move.

*   *   *

3:00 p.m. (EST)—Mills stood up from his position at the head of the table. Around him sat five men who represented the bulk of the people who could supply him with the information he was seeking.

"I need to know if anything is going on of any consequence whatsoever," he began.

The man in charge of the Western Europe operations spoke up. "I was just told about an hour ago by my sources that the KGB is becoming much more active over in my area. It's like they're throwing a huge spider web over the area trying to snag someone or something."

"Okay, gentlemen, I don't need to remind anyone that what I'm about to tell you is classified as top secret. My guess is that the man they're trying to capture may be the one we're looking for too."

*   *   *

Day Three—Elaina's trip thankfully proved to be more uneventful than she had first imagined. The space she was afforded was anything but comfortable, the only luxury being the small pillow to rest her head on. Only the gaps between the boards that admitted air and the occasional glimpses of light convinced her she was not in a coffin. At the same time, she was impressed with the structure of the hiding place. It would survive any cursory examination of the truck.

She could not be aware that the route she was on took her through Kiev and had entered Romania through the small border town Mihaileni just south of Chervovsky. Along the way they had made several stops, a few long enough for Elaina to relieve her bladder, which at times felt as if it would burst. At one location, the truck was stopped by some guards who, evidently, the truck driver was on friendly terms with (evidenced by the conversation and laughter between him and the soldiers). After resuming their journey, she listened while the unseen driver explained how the military often provided for vehicles to have unhampered transportation through certain areas in exchange for items being transported.

On the second solid day of driving, the truck finally came to a halt. The driver stepped out of the vehicle and gave her one final order. "Wait here until you are told what to do next."

Elaina judged by the diminishing light that evening was fast approaching, and finally, she found herself totally in the dark. In the distance, she could hear the faint lapping of water.

Gradually, fear set in, which slowly began to transform itself into phobia. A thousand different scenarios, each one more frightening than the previous, ran through her mind. What if the driver was caught and forced to tell them of my whereabouts? In her mind, the compartment began to shrink as a degree of claustrophobia began to set in. She found herself sobbing, and only by sheer determination was she able to stop. And then, her ears picked up the sound of footsteps walking across gravel and around to the back of the truck. She could hear the tailgate being lowered and someone climbing into the back of the truck. Whoever it was, he was having a difficult time in maneuvering through the stacks of boxes that filled the truck, judging by the mild oaths she could overhear.

Then she heard a soft voice speaking in broken English. "Wait thirty seconds, and then open the trap door. When you get out of the truck, you will see a boat tied up on the dock. Get into the cabin of the boat, and someone will be with you soon to take you on the next part of your journey."

With those instructions, the voice faded into silence, and she could hear the footsteps exiting the truck. Elaina did as she was told and counted to thirty. One-one thousand, two-one thousand . . . After reaching thirty, Elaina unlocked the latch and quickly climbed out of her jail. No prisoner could have felt any more a sense of freedom than what she experienced. The man who had spoken to her was nowhere in sight. Quickly, she clambered out of the truck and took a survey of her surroundings. There was no moon out, and only the stars and a small naked bulb attached to a tattered, corrugated iron building provided her with any light with which to see. As she had initially surmised, she was near a large body of water. There was a small dock, and tied to it was a fishing boat that she judged to be approximately thirty-five or forty feet in length. Following the instructions she had been given, she walked quickly over to the wooden dock and climbed into the boat where she waited in silence and in the dark. She could barely make out the features inside the cabin, which appeared to be basically stark. The front of the wheelhouse contained several buttons on a wooden panel along with the controls necessary to steer the vessel. Behind was a wall with a small door, evidently leading to sleeping quarters below.

Suddenly, she heard the sounds of the door being opened and she became aware that someone had just entered the cabin. As her eyes became more adjusted to the dark, Elaina could make out a small man in front of her. He was shorter that her, wiry, and probably in his midsixties. He turned on a small light inside the cabin, and she noticed his calloused hands (which she surmised were from a lifetime of fishing) and a stubble of beard on his deeply lined face, indicating he had not shaved for several days. But what caught her attention the most were his eyes. They almost twinkled in merriment.

He spoke to her in what was obviously his native tongue, which she did not understand. She gave him a blank stare and shrugged her shoulders.

"Well," he said, smiling, "my English is not so good, but it is much better than my Russian. Are you ready to go?"

"I think so," she replied. "But where are we?"

"Where we are is not important, but where we are going is," he said, pointing across the water. "Tomorrow, I will put you ashore on the coast of Italy, and from there, you will be expected to get to Rome on your own. Until then, you can lie down and try to rest. There is a bed down below."

He pressed a button on the panel, and she could feel the engine underneath her feet shudder briefly before springing to life. Stepping out of the cabin, the man untied the two ropes that tied the boat to the dock. Engaging the engine into gear, he turned the bow of the boat in a southwesterly direction at a speed of fifteen knots.

Elaina suddenly became aware of how tired she was, realizing how little restful sleep she had managed to get since she had left Moscow. Thanking her newest benefactor, she climbed down the steps and lay down on the small bed. The freedom of movement she now enjoyed did as much for her mentally as it did physically, and she managed a smile for the first time in many days, believing her future now looked much more promising. Tomorrow, if things went well, she would be inside the safe confines of the American embassy in Rome. The gentle movement of the boat rocked her into oblivion.

Chapter Six

Day Four—*AP midday news—For only the second time in its history, the Dow Jones has suspended trading after the market fell more than six hundred points in the first two-and-a-half hours. The automatic trigger to halt trading is done with the hope that nervous traders will have their fears eased before trading resumes at 9:00 a.m. tomorrow.*

*   *   *

"Who did you tell? What did you tell them? Tell me what I want to know, or I'll cut your fingers one by one!" said the man holding the menacing knife. "Where are the papers?"

"Here!" screamed Elaina.

The man laughed, grabbing her hand. She screamed again.

She sat up in her bed, shrieking at the top of her lungs. It was only then she realized she had been in a nightmare. It was broad daylight, and she rose to her feet, feeling refreshed from a fitful sleep. She stepped out of the cabin and found herself staring out at an empty ocean.

"Where are we?" she asked.

"About two hours from the Italian coast," the man replied. "Are you all right?"

Elaina nodded. "I just had a bad dream. I'll be fine. Who is steering the boat?" she wondered aloud, suddenly nervous again.

"Do not worry, young lady," he laughed. "It is on automatic pilot."

They walked out on the deck. In every direction there was only water, except to the southwest. On the horizon, she could just make out the clear outline of a ship. The fisherman followed her gaze.

"That is the ferry that runs from Dubrovnik to Bari," he commented. "We will land a little north of there between two coastal towns, Bisceglie and Molfetta. You can catch a bus going north from either place. When you get to

Pescara, you will change buses that will take you into Rome from there. Most all of the taxi drivers speak English, so you will not have any problems getting to where you want to go."

"What do I use for money?" Elaina asked. "I have none."

"Follow me," he said, leading her back into the wheelhouse. He opened a cabinet and removed a small packet from two old canisters.

"Here are one hundred thousand lira and five thousand in United States dollars. That should be more than enough to get you by. But first, we need to take care of your identification."

Walking over to the steering wheel, he reached under the decking and pulled out an ancient Polaroid camera, a wooden box, and a small bottle of what appeared to be glue. He then motioned for Elaina to stand over by the back of the cabin, reached above her, and pulled down a white roll of paper about six feet wide. Using it as a background, he then positioned himself in front of Elaina and took several pictures of his subject. After they had developed, he studied them carefully before selecting the one he felt would best suit his purpose. Opening the box, he next removed a pair of scissors and a small document that appeared to be about four-by-six inches. Using the scissors with practiced hands, he cut Elaina's picture into the dimensions he wanted. Opening up the document, he affixed the picture to the first page using the gluey substance and then handed it to Elaina.

Elaina looked at the document in amazement. "It-it looks so authentic," she stammered.

"It is authentic," he answered proudly. "Those are a genuine Russian passport and visa. I understand it does not take much these days to obtain them. And the visa has already been stamped with both Italian and United States seals."

Elaina impulsively leaned over, gave him a hug, and kissed him on the cheek as tears welled up in her eyes. "I don't know how to thank you, all of you. If it were not for your help . . ."

The rest of the sentence was caught up in her throat.

The fisherman returned her embrace. "Words are not necessary, my young friend. We all work for the same goals. Besides, your gratitude can best be expressed by getting the information you possess to the people who can use it. Now try to relax if you can. We will be on the Italian coast soon."

*   *   *

The fisherman had taken Elaina into a deserted part of the coastline as close as he dared before dropping her off in relatively shallow water. Her clothing was totally soaked by the time she reached land, and although the sun had quickly dried it off, her natural vanity felt it would be necessary to obtain new material before traveling any farther. Her money, passport, and a pair of sandals had been kept dry in a waterproof pouch attached to her skirt. After she had reached land, she had donned the sandals. The rest she had transferred into a small purse that he had also provided.

Elaina found the road easily and began the short walk into the town of Molfetta. Her first order of business was to make herself more presentable, partly out of vanity but mostly out of necessity. The clothes she had been wearing for the last three days were beginning to deteriorate, and she had no desire to bring any unwanted attention upon herself. A brief stop at a clothing store in the small town met her needs quite satisfactorily. Besides a new sundress and undergarments, she also purchased a sun hat, some makeup, a small bottle of inexpensive perfume, and a large purse to replace the small one in her possession. She walked out of the store feeling much refreshed. She did not notice the saleslady gleefully counting the extra five thousand lira she had managed to extract from the ignorant tourista, nor would Elaina have cared had she known.

She had some difficulty in getting directions to the bus station until a young ten-year-old boy who spoke a smattering of English offered to take her there himself. When they arrived, she turned to offer her thanks and found herself staring at his outstretched hand. She again pulled out the wad of bills, not sure what to give him. Not bothering to count it, she took out several bills and handed them to him. Much to her relief, he smiled broadly and ran off in the other direction, leaving her alone at the station. Elaina went inside to purchase a ticket from the elderly man behind the counter, and as fortune would have it, a bus pulled up to the building barely fifteen minutes later with the name *Pescara* in bold letters on its front. Inside, the bus was not overly crowded, and she felt fortunate to find a seat with no one next to her. During the ride, she began thinking about the message she had sent and who the receiver was. Her CIA handler had impressed upon her the critical nature of escape if it became necessary, and she had studied the information he had supplied until it had become etched into her memory.

At Pescara, she made the transfer to the bus bound for Rome. The second bus was much more crowded than the first, and she was forced to spend the majority of her time listening to a bunch of women conversing in Italian. The arrival at the bus station into Rome late that afternoon came without incident. Elaina's biggest concern lay with her fear that her enemy would be waiting for her when she stepped off. A careful scrutiny of the crowd from the bus window, however, did not reveal any suspicious-looking people, and she stepped off hoping she could blend into the throng of people surrounding her.

She had barely stepped off, however, when she felt a hand tap her on her shoulder. Startled, Elaina spun around, ready to scream at the top of her lungs, only to find herself facing a small elderly man.

"Forgive me, signora," he apologized. "I do not mean to startle you. I only wish to offer you the services of the finest taxi and the best driver in Rome."

Elaina's look changed to one of relief. "Can you take me to the U.S. Embassy?" she asked after gathering her thoughts.

"I can take a beautiful lady such as yourself anywhere in Rome," he grinned. "Please come this way."

With that, he led her to a nearby Fiat and opened a door for her. After she was comfortably seated, he closed the door. He then quickly walked around to his side of the car, hopped in behind the wheel, and started the engine.

Elaina had never experienced such a wild ride in a car before. Her driver, who identified himself as Marco, constantly sounded his horn and, seemingly without looking, darted in and out among the cars amidst the sounds of screeching brakes and other car horns blaring around him. If he was concerned, he showed no outward signs of it. Instead, during the majority of the ride, he kept up a lively monologue with his passenger, pointing out various sights and landmarks as they passed by. Elaina tried her best to appear interested although her thoughts were elsewhere. She noticed after about twenty minutes of driving that the traffic began noticeably to thin out. It was only then that she saw that she was surrounded by a series of large homes with different flags flying in front of them. She smiled, knowing that her flight to freedom was about to end. As she peered in front of the taxi, she spotted the United States flag several houses down. As Marco was about to pull over in front of the building, Elaina caught something out of the corner of her eye that caused the hairs on the back of her neck to stand on end.

Inside a car opposite the embassy were two men staring intently at them as they passed by, and Elaina found herself looking directly at one of them. Instinctively, she knew she was staring at the eyes of a KGB agent. She grabbed Marco by his shoulder.

"Please, don't stop," she whispered in terror. "Keep going."

Her driver glanced behind him curiously but did as instructed, pulling back into the street and accelerating. "Are you all right, signora?" he asked with genuine concern in his voice.

Elaina looked behind her as the KGB car pulled out and then turned around to look at Marco.

"Please go faster," she pleaded. "I need to trust you to do something for me, Marco," she began as he picked up speed. "Those men in the car behind us, they want to hurt me—or even worse. Can you help me?"

Marco laughed. "Do not worry, signora. Not only will I lose them in this traffic, they will be lost themselves when the chase is over. Watch what I am about to do."

"But they are gaining on us," Elaina said in fear.

"That is what I want them to do," he said with a big grin.

Her driver first moved the taxi into the traffic of a major three-lane, one-way thoroughfare with the pursuing car following only a few yards behind them. He then positioned the vehicle in the far right-hand lane. With his eyes peering intently into his side-view mirror, he suddenly darted to his left across both of the other two lanes of traffic and into a smaller side street. The driver behind them was caught totally unawares and had to come to a complete halt. The drivers whom he had cut off so drastically slammed on their brakes momentarily to avoid a collision before blaring their horns in displeasure and then continuing on. The driver in the pursuing car could only watch helplessly as traffic moved past him to the left. It was only after the drivers in the cars behind him began to honk their horns impatiently that he had to admit defeat and go forward. Thankfully, Elaina watched through the rear window as her followers faded from sight. She knew she had escaped another brush with death.

* * *

Day Five, noon (EST)—*UPI midday news*—*"The Dow has fallen over five hundred points since the opening bell this morning. Analysts attribute much of the fall to the fact that news has leaked this morning that several money center banks in New York are having computer-related problems with some of the accounts of their large corporate customers. At this point, the banks have been unable or unwilling to offer any suggestions as to whether this is a problem related to Y2K or if there is any criminal activity involved. Elsewhere in the country, it has been reported that a bank employee in a small town in Texas was shot and critically wounded this morning when an enraged bank customer was unable to withdraw funds from his bank account. An official of the First National Bank of Hempstead told reporters that eighty-eight-year-old Brian Miller had gone through the bank's drive-in and asked for all of the money in both his savings and checking accounts. When told by the teller at the window that the bank did not have the money with which to comply with his request, he evidently drove home and returned with a gun. He walked into the bank lobby and made the request for a second time. When told by the inside teller that too many people had come in earlier to do the same thing and, as a result, there were insufficient funds to meet his demand, in a fit of evident rage, he shot the teller in the chest, screaming that the bank wasn't going to steal his money again like they did seventy-five years ago. Another quick-thinking customer managed to tackle Mr. Miller and wrestle him to the ground where he was quickly subdued and handcuffed by an off-duty policeman. An elderly witness, who asked not to be identified, said the incident was reminiscent of the run on banks in 1929 and the resulting stock market crash. Bank officials have assured its customers that more funds are being sent to the bank to avert any future problems. In a related story, the Fed announced this morning that it is printing an additional 800 billion dollars to prevent any future similar incidents from occurring. It has also promised its member banks that those who are federally chartered will be able to receive federal assistance within twenty-four hours, if needed. It is also making similar arrangements to help those banks that are chartered by the states. Indications are, however, that despite this guarantee, much of the public remains skeptical."*

*   *   *

Jonathan walked out of the men's restroom and bent over the water fountain to get a drink. It was then that he became acutely aware of several pairs of eyes that were staring at him. H spun around quickly to find several secretaries doing their best to look away. He descended on the nearest one.

"Lady," he said testily, "I hope I'm not keeping you from your work."

The sharp tone of his voice caught the woman off guard.

"I'm sorry, sir," she managed to say. "I didn't mean to—"

"Well, you did," Jonathan snapped. "Maybe you and your friends would like me to provide you with a daily report on what we're doing if you're so curious."

The woman, who appeared to be in her midtwenties, looked as if she might start crying.

"Now don't you pull those tears on me," Jonathan said in an angry tone. "The only thing we want is to be left alone without feeling like we're carrying the plague around wherever we go. We've got better things to do than to walk around on eggshells so that we can keep this bank from hemorrhaging to death!"

As he was finishing his sentence, Walker felt a strong grip underneath his arm. He spun around to find himself face to face with Doug.

"And I'm sure these people have got better things to do than listen to some idiot make a fool of himself in the middle of the lobby," he remarked icily. "Pardon us, ladies. My friend here hasn't made it out of obedience school with a passing grade yet. Please follow me, Mr. Walker, back to our room. We don't want to ruin any more of their day, do we?"

With that comment, Doug forced Jonathan back into the room they were occupying. Once inside, he slammed the door and angrily faced his friend.

"What has gotten into you?" he demanded. "Those people know something's wrong, and nobody's telling them anything. Have you seen their faces? They're probably wondering if they're going to have a job next week, and you turn around and make some comment about the bank hemorrhaging. Good grief!"

Jonathan turned and walked over to the table where their work was spread out. "I'm sorry, okay!" he said. "I'm just tired of feeling I'm under a microscope every time I go out of the room."

"You're tired!" Doug retorted. "What do you think is going through their minds right now? Do you have any idea how they feel? You can bet your next paycheck that your comment is going to be all over this building by the end of the day!"

Jonathan paused for a brief moment. "I'm sorry," he said in a low tone.

"Don't tell me!" Doug snapped at him. "I'm not the person you just walked all over a few minutes ago." With that, he went over to his chair and continued reviewing the file in front of him.

Jonathan stood by himself for what seemed like an eternity before swallowing his pride and walking over to the door.

Taking a deep breath, he opened it and walked over to the secretary he had berated moments before.

"My friend was right," he began softly. "I am an idiot, and there's no excuse for my bad behavior a few minutes ago. I can only ask for your forgiveness—not only for what I said to you but also for my comment about the bank. I just let some personal issues back home cloud my judgment. If there's anything I can do or say to make it up to you, please let me know, okay?"

No one spoke. Jonathan stood for a moment before turning around and walking back to his office. Inside, Doug had the phone next to his ear and was motioning to him in a frenzied manner.

"What's going on?" Jonathan asked.

"Grab your jacket," Doug replied. "There's someone downstairs who wants to talk to us. I think we're about to find out the real reason why we're here."

$$* \quad * \quad *$$

Elaina had to do a quick reevaluation of her situation as Marco drove off. She watched with relief as he left her pursuers far behind. Returning to the U.S. embassy was now out of the question as she was convinced it would be under constant surveillance. After some thought, she instructed Marco to take her to a women's clothing shop. When he pulled up in front of one, she got out of the taxi. She reached into her purse to pay the fare, but when he asked her if he could wait for her, she bent down at the driver's window and shook her head.

"The men who are following me know your license number, Marco," she said. "I must use another taxi to get where I need to go. But I want to thank you for helping me get away."

She handed him several thousand lira and smiled.

"As you wish, signora," he nodded. "Good luck."

Elaina turned around as Marco drove off and walked into the store. Once inside, she quickly located the department that had wigs on display and selected one with a color and length that she felt would alter her appearance enough to fool most people but not so flamboyant as to draw attention to herself. On impulse, she also decided to further upgrade her wardrobe by purchasing a business suit, some extra undergarments, a briefcase, a wrist watch and a pair of expensive sunglasses that had the effect of darkening and brightening depending on the amount of outside light. That way, she felt confident she could comfortably move around in open spaces. After changing her clothes in one of the dressing rooms provided, she stepped out and viewed herself in a full-length mirror, totally confident she could easily pass as a businesswoman.

Elaina asked the store clerk if there was a nearby place where she could purchase airline tickets in advance. The clerk nodded in the affirmative and, in her best English, told her customer that there was a nearby business three blocks down the street. Elaina thanked her and, after paying for her merchandise, walked down to her next destination. Finding a man in an open cubicle, Elaina told him she wanted to purchase a ticket into New York City as quickly as possible. The agent on the other side of the desk, who spoke excellent English, tried to interest her in other features in hopes of getting a bigger commission on the transaction, but Elaina assured him that all of her business would be conducted in New York. When he asked her if he could at least book her for a return flight, she told him she was not sure how long she would be staying and said that a one-way ticket would suffice. Obviously disappointed, he nevertheless yielded and processed her request in short order. He told her that United Airlines was the only U.S. carrier that flew directly from Da Vinci into New York and that the next flight would not be leaving until ten the following morning, and because of the time zone changes, she would arrive at her destination approximately noon the same day. She asked her agent about airport security, and though puzzled by the query, he assured her that the passenger area was well protected and that only those with tickets were allowed past a certain point. Elaina walked out feeling quite satisfied with herself. However, she remained skeptical about sleeping at the airport, and so she found an inexpensive hotel close by. The night seemed to drag on interminably, but at last, sunlight began to filter into her room. Elaina rose, and after showering, she quickly dressed and made her way out the front door of the hotel and grabbed a taxi. She instructed her driver to take her to the airport and sat back to relax as best as she could. In less than twenty minutes, the cab pulled up in front of terminal 5, and after paying her fare, Elaina took a deep breath and stepped out of the vehicle. She remembered that she was playing the part of a business individual and did her best to put on an air of confidence as she strolled through the glass door.

Despite the high fees that were being charged due to soaring fuel prices, it evidently was doing little to slow airline traffic. This pleased Elaina as it provided her an extra layer of protection from prying eyes, which she was sure were concealed inside the terminal. She glanced at her watch, hoping to time her passage through the security checkpoint in order to walk immediately on to her flight. She next glanced at the TV monitors above her to verify her plane was still scheduled as on time. Thirty minutes before the scheduled departure, Elaina walked up to the security desk. She had no carry-on luggage, and since she had provided the documentation for a quick preflight boarding back with the agent who had booked her passage, she was quickly whisked through.

Elaina tried to time the pace of her steps as she walked into the waiting area. But when she saw that people were already gathering at the gate, she hurried to get in line. She was relieved when a female voice announced less than a minute later that passengers could begin boarding. She handed her boarding pass to the flight attendant and walked up the ramp to the Boeing 737. Inside, she was greeted by a smiling stewardess and shown to her seat. After putting her briefcase into an overhead compartment, she gladly slumped down into her seat. She felt tired from getting little sleep from the night before, and she gladly accepted a pillow when her stewardess offered one. Elaina vaguely remembered the captain's voice coming over the intercom but was sound asleep before the huge wheels of the aircraft lifted off the ground.

It was well for Elaina's peace of mind that she was not aware that her passage through the security gate had been observed by two pairs of eyes belonging to the KGB. They took note of the woman who closely fit the description of their quarry and dutifully reported it to other men who, in turn, would have someone waiting at Dulles when the flight landed.

Chapter Seven

"So what gives?" Jonathan demanded.

"I don't want to ruin the surprise," Doug answered. "Let's just say that there's someone downstairs who wants to speak to us and leave it at that. Okay?"

The two stepped off the elevator and walked through the revolving door on to the street. Doug pointed to a big Lincoln Continental limousine with darkened windows and headed in that direction. As they neared the vehicle, the driver stepped out of the car. He opened the rear door and, without speaking, motioned Jonathan and Doug to climb inside. Jonathan was hesitant at first, but Doug wasted no time. After Jonathan had entered the car, the door was shut behind them.

The driver got behind the wheel and pulled away from the curb. Jonathan sat in the seat and looked up to find himself staring at Alan Greenberg, chairman of the Federal Reserve, and a man seated next to him whose identity he was not familiar with.

Jonathan was caught briefly off guard before regrouping his thoughts. "Good afternoon, Mr. Chairman," he said. "I'm sorry if I seem somewhat taken aback. Doug told me there was someone downstairs who wanted to talk to us, but I wasn't ready to meet such a high-profile individual as yourself."

"I'm used to it." Greenberg smiled. "Gentlemen, I'd like for you to meet Mr. Robert Mills, head of the CIA."

Neither Jonathan nor Doug was prepared to learn of the man's identity who had, to this point, remained silent.

"Mr. Warner, Mr. Walker," he said, extending his hand. "It's a pleasure to meet you. Mr. Greenberg here has told me a lot about you two. I must say I'm quite impressed with the things he has told me about you."

Jonathan looked slightly uncomfortable.

"Don't necessarily believe everything you hear," Doug grinned.

"Oh, that's okay," Mills replied. "I did a little checking on you myself on the way over from JFK. You two lead the FDIC in criminals convicted of bank fraud. But I am just a little curious. Which of you is called Rambo, and which is called Robocop?"

Greenberg couldn't help but chuckle. "I hadn't heard about that. But I think it's safe to say that I think we have the right two men for what we're about to discuss. First of all, the reason I'm here is that I found out from someone at the Houston office named Mark Duncan that you two were the ones up here in New York and the ones that I needed to talk to. I've been in contact with Mr. Mills for the last few days, and when I found out he was flying up here to New York, I made a snap decision to join him. I don't like to fly commercial in the current climate—too many people know my face. So I had a man drive all night from DC to get here and meet him at the airport."

"And by the way," Mills said in a more serious tone, "what I'm—we're—about to talk to you about is considered a matter of national importance. Top secret. Please do not repeat this to anyone—and I mean anyone. Not Mark Duncan, not your wives, no one."

During the next thirty minutes, Greenberg and Mills began laying out everything that had transpired over the last four or five days. When they had finished, Doug and Jonathan looked at each other.

"I guess this explains a lot of things—why we've been spinning our wheels ever since we got here," Doug said. "We've been looking at bank files until we're blue in the face, and there's nothing wrong with them—at least nothing that an infusion of equity into the companies couldn't fix. And none of the secretaries know what's going on any more than we did until a few minutes ago. They just know something's not kosher, and they're scared."

"So you think someone in the KGB has figured out how to hack into our banks," said Jonathan. "Well, it would be a great way of causing chaos. Look what's happening on Wall Street. It's in a free fall tumble right now, and John Q. Public still doesn't fully know what's happened."

"It probably has something to do with their top guy," said Mills. "His name is Kheraskov. And he's one sadistic man. Don't ever cross him. He will do whatever it takes to get what he wants, and it's never pleasant."

"The CEOs at the banks can't keep a lid on this for much longer," remarked Greenberg. "If we can't find out what happened to the money and get it back, there's going to be utter panic in the streets all across America. And if that happens, you can kiss this country good-bye. I figure we can keep things under wraps for a couple of weeks max. But as you've seen in the news, the investors on Wall Street can feel that something's not kosher. And it's going to get a lot worse before it gets better."

"Well," said Doug, "to begin with, there had to be some help both on the inside and outside to pull something like this off. Those banks all have freestanding computer systems. I can't help you with the ones on the outside, but I'd get a list of every person from every one of those banks who's been hired in their computer rooms for the last fifteen or twenty years. See if any of them has mysteriously vanished in the last few days."

"Consider it done," said Greenberg.

At that moment, Mills's cell phone rang.

* * *

Elaina awoke with a start as she felt a gentle hand shaking her shoulder. She looked up to find her stewardess smiling down at her.

"I didn't want to wake you until the last minute, ma'am," she said, "but we'll be landing in New York in about an hour. Can I get you anything before we land?"

Elaina thought for a moment as she tried to regain her faculties. "Is there some way I could borrow a cell phone before we land?" she asked. "There's someone I need to talk to, if that would be possible. And I'll be glad to reimburse someone for their trouble. I have a thousand dollars in U.S. currency."

She pulled out her purse, opened it, and counted out ten one-hundred-dollar bills.

"I don't think we'll have any problem finding someone willing to help you." The stewardess laughed. "I'll be right back."

She moved forward about three rows and leaned over to speak to another passenger. Whatever she said had the effect of having the man she spoke to turn his head and glance back in her direction. With a smile, he handed the stewardess his phone. She then walked back to Elaina and turned the device over to her.

"Can I go back to the bathroom to make my call?" Elaina asked. "It's rather personal."

"That shouldn't be a problem, ma'am," the stewardess replied.

Elaina thanked the woman and excused herself. She walked to the back of the cabin and stepped into one of the lavatories marked Unoccupied. Inside the cramped space, she made herself as comfortable as possible, opened the cell phone, and hit the number zero.

A woman's voice came on the other end. "What city, please?"

"Langley, Virginia."

There was a pause as the call was redirected.

"How may I help you?" came another voice.

"I'd like to speak to someone at the Central Intelligence Agency, please," Elaina said.

There was another pause followed by several rings. A man's voice came across the line. "CIA," he said in a somewhat bored voice.

"I have some very important information that I need to speak to one of your agents about," Elaina said in a subdued voice.

"Perhaps you would like to leave a message on one of our answering machines," the man said, as if he had heard the same story before.

"Please, sir," Elaina said as she gripped her phone. "Don't hang up. My name is Elaina Grigoriev. Five days ago, I sent someone at the CIA a FLASH message regarding the assassination of President Constanza and a banking conspiracy. I was a mole in Russia until a man caught me listening to a secret meeting, and now Dimitri Kheraskov, who is in charge of the KGB, is trying to kill me. Please don't disconnect me."

Perhaps it was the desperation in Elaina's voice that caused the man to acquiesce, but there were not too many people outside the CIA who knew the name of Dimitri Kheraskov, and after a brief pause, he rerouted her call.

*   *   *

Robert Mills listened for a few minutes and then hung up his cell phone. "Well, if you two have nothing pressing right now, there's someone you might be interested in meeting," he said. "I understand our Russian mole will be landing at JFK in about thirty or forty minutes. And it's a woman, by the way."

Greenberg gave instructions to the driver on where to take them and then said, "I'll just stay out here in the car while you three go inside and get her."

The limousine arrived at JFK about ten minutes ahead of the flight. When they stepped out, a policeman who was directing traffic approached them and was about to ask the driver to move when Mills flashed his badge in his direction. The policeman took one look at Mills's credentials and immediately retreated to his previous position. Mills nodded at Jonathan and Doug, and the three walked into the terminal.

*   *   *

Elaina was feeling quite satisfied with her situation. The man with whom she had been speaking had placed her on hold for a few brief minutes and returned to tell her that a man would be meeting her at the terminal when she exited the plane. He gave the name of her contact and a description of what Mills looked like and then hung up the phone. Before returning to her seat, she walked forward to hand the man his cell phone and thanked him for its use. Twenty minutes later, she heard the deep rumbling of the landing gear being lowered and the captain's voice instructing his passengers to return to their seats. Shortly thereafter, she felt the wheels of the jet touch down on the tarmac.

The moment the Unbuckle Seatbelt lights came on, Elaina was out of her seat and had quickly grabbed her briefcase from the overhead compartment. To her annoyance, there were a number of people in front of her who were evidently in an equal hurry to deplane, and she had to wait for the line to slowly thin out. When it finally did, she quickly followed everyone off the plane and immediately began looking around in search of her contact. Mills, Walker, and Warner—who were waiting among a group of people—immediately spotted their target, and Mills raised his hand to get her attention.

Elaina smiled and immediately headed in his direction. "You must be Mr. Mills," she said. "I'm so happy to meet you. It's been so long since I've felt this safe."

"And I take it you must be Elaina Grigoriev," Mills replied as they headed for the waiting car. "Your communication has caused quite a stir. By the way, I'd like you to meet Messrs. Walker and Warner. They work for the Federal Deposit Insurance Corporation and will try to help figure out what is going on from the banking end of the equation. I am curious about one aspect of your transmission, however. What was the question mark about?"

"It happened right as that man found me listening in on the meeting. Kheraskov was about to introduce someone to his people. It sounded like he said 'Oba' or something like that. And then he said that he had one more little surprise that was going to happen on the twenty-third of—"

At that moment, Elaina stopped suddenly in her tracks. Mills turned around to see her staring into space, an ominous red spot appearing on the upper right part of her chest and growing rapidly. She collapsed onto the tile flooring, blood starting to pool and spread onto the floor. A woman screamed.

*　　*　　*

Kheraskov was livid with rage. Much of his plan was unraveling before his eyes. "Where is he?" he demanded.

"The driver who took him to the airport said that his flight was to New York," Musorgski answered. "No one has seen him since."

"Find him—now," Kheraskov ordered. "I want him found—now! Use whatever means necessary. Find out what he did with the money. With it, I will be the next premiere of the Soviet Union, and the United States will be unable to stop me. As I predicted, America is now in the process of destroying itself."

*　　*　　*

"You missed!" hissed the man to his partner as they hurried off.

"It was not my fault!" answered the other, equally angry. "Someone hit me from behind as I was squeezing the trigger. In case you haven't noticed, the airport is crowded."

"Let's get out of here and find out who the other two with Mills were," said the first. "Kheraskov is going to be mad enough as it is. Maybe we soothe his anger with some important information."

*   *   *

Mills assessed the situation quickly. He pulled out the gun that he carried holstered underneath his coat and surveyed everyone in near proximity. Unable to locate a gunman, he turned his attention back to Elaina.

"Someone get a doctor!" he yelled "This woman has been shot!"

Jonathan looked around quickly, but not finding anything that suited his purpose, he took off his jacket, tore off his shirt, and handed it to Mills.

"Here," he said. "Use this for a bandage until help gets here."

A man came running up to them and bent down next to Elaina on one knee. He gently rolled her over on her side to look at her back before laying her on her back again. "I'm a doctor," he said as he examined her. "We need to let the medics here at the airport know that we appear to have a through-and-through gunshot wound. She's breathing, and it's good that she's not coughing up any blood, so the bullet appears to have missed her lungs."

Mills looked up at Jonathan and Doug and gave them specific instructions. "You two need to get out of here and back to the car before some reporter shows up and starts asking a lot of questions. I'm going to stay with Ms. Grigoriev until we get her to the hospital. I'm also going to need and make sure that she gets round-the-clock protection from some of my people while she's there. Obviously, someone wants her dead. Tell Greenberg what happened, and head on back to your office. I'll call if I need you for anything. And Jonathan"—he smiled—"make sure you stop off somewhere and get a new shirt. I'm sure the people at the office would appreciate it."

Jonathan and Doug were hurrying off as two paramedics on a golf cart were arriving. Two airport policemen were also running on to the scene. Doug saw Mills flash his badge to one of the officers and heard him give instructions to have the immediate area cleared and to watch out for any suspicious onlookers. Taking Mills's instruction to heart, they made their way back to where Greenberg was waiting. When they informed him of what had happened, he quickly instructed his driver to vacate the airport premises as he did not want any shrewd reporter or other individual to be made aware of his presence. None of them noticed the car directly behind that was discreetly following them.

"I called the bank CEOs while you were in the airport, and I got a response from four of them so far," Greenberg said. "As you suspected, each one of them is reporting that one employee has disappeared. Where to—they don't know. I've instructed someone from my office to call the chief of police here in New York City and put an all-points bulletin on every one of them although I have little faith they'll be found anytime soon."

"Well, now that we know what we need to look for, Doug will get on it as soon as we get back to the bank," said Jonathan.

"And what special gifts do you have to handle this situation?" Greenberg asked with a touch of curiosity.

"Well," Doug said, "I think what Jonathan means is that whoever orchestrated this thing probably did his best to cover his tracks by wiping out anything on the various computer systems that would tell us where the funds were electronically transferred to. My forte is that I'm one of those computer geeks who knows how to invade the deep logic of a computer and dig things up that criminals may have left behind. What I will try to do is reconstruct one of the computers back to the point where the transfer took place. Then we can find out the routing number of the bank that received the funds. After that, it'll be up to someone on your side of the equation to take over."

"How long will it take you?" Greenberg asked.

"Max effort," said Doug thoughtfully, "I'm going to guess no more than twelve hours. Just make sure I have unfettered access to the computer room back at the bank and someone who can help me."

"I hope you're that good," said Greenberg. "We're running out of time. The banks can't keep a lid on this much longer."

"Believe me when I tell you he's that good," Jonathan said with confidence. "As Doug once told me, the money can run, but it can't hide. What I've got to do while Doug is doing his thing is prepare an interim report to send to Mark Duncan back at our office and let him know where we're at in the investigation. But I promise you that I'll leave out any mention of what you and Mr. Mills don't want us to talk about. I'm also going to send a copy of the report to my house by Federal Express as a backup, but it won't have any of the information that you don't want open to the public. I'll make sure my wife doesn't even open the envelope so our secret will be safe."

*　　*　　*

The elderly man walked into his hotel room, only a floor above the one where he had just completed his gruesome task. The inside had held a Do Not Disturb sign on it for several days now, and its appearance had undertaken a dramatic transformation. A knowledgeable person would have recognized it as having the appearance of a miniature Shinto shrine half a world away. Walking quietly, he passed the statues of two Komainu, one on each side of the door. He slowly removed his business clothing, put on a formal white robe, and then knelt down on both knees. A trained eye would have noticed the bulge in the right pocket of his jacket. Seven others had not. In this case, there was no *kaishahunin* (or assistant) to help complete his task. What needed to be done, he knew, would have to be done by him. A bottle of sake, an empty cup, and a piece of paper containing a poem of death he had written sat on the small coffee table. The man picked up the bottle with his left hand, poured it from the left side, and placed the bottle back down. Picking up the paper and reading the poem done in the waka style, he contemplated the wording that reflected his love for his parents, sister, and wife—all dead, either directly or indirectly, from the blast of 1945. He then prayed for forgiveness of the deed he had just finished committing and all of the other sins he could think of. Mitsuru Obah had made up his mind many years earlier that, while the United States would pay for the deaths of his family, he would not be giving Kheraskov the satisfaction of having the funds either. Kheraskov did not know it, but he despised the Soviet Union nearly as much by what it had represented for so many years.

After his prayer was complete, he set the paper down and picked up the sake cup. Lifting the cup to his lips he emptied the contents in two drinks, not one that he might demonstrate greed or more than two to show hesitation. Finishing the ceremonial drink, he then set the cup down. Beside him on the carpet lay the *kozuka* blade inside its sheath. Drawing the sharpened blade out, he raised it above his head with both hands, firmly gripping it, and brought the sharp instrument swiftly down in one final thrust. Before lapsing into unconsciousness, he twisted the hilt, confident his secret would now die with him.

Chapter Eight

After stopping to buy Jonathan a new shirt, Greenberg dropped him and Doug off back at the bank.

"I don't think Greenberg was too keen on the idea of you sending a copy of the report back to your house," Doug grinned.

"I don't care," replied Jonathan. "I'm not going to get burned again by the post office just because they lost my report in the mail. I got reamed by Mark when it wasn't ready to go to DC the last time. It's not going to happen again."

"What I need to get is the SWIFT number," said Doug. "Whoever did this isn't going to put three-and-a-half trillion dollars in a bank around here. There'd be red flags going up all over the place. Ergo, it would have to go somewhere outside the country, to a place where they value secrecy above all else."

"Like Switzerland?" Jonathan asked.

"Like Switzerland," Doug nodded. "I'll be spending most of my time in the computer room. I bet I'll have the information before we head back to the hotel this evening. And by the way, it's good to have you back among the living again."

"I guess understanding why they dragged us out of Houston makes a little sense now," Jonathan agreed. "I'll make you a friendly wager. I bet you don't have the SWIFT code before nine this evening. Loser buys the hamburgers."

"You're on," answered Doug. "When you lose, I'd like mine with no pickles or onions."

The elevator stopped at the fourth floor where the computer room was located. Doug stepped off as Jonathan left him with a parting shot. "You have four hours and thirty-seven minutes to find that SWIFT number, or you owe me a hamburger."

*   *   *

"Did you get all of that?" the driver asked his companion who was pointing the listening device at the limousine in front of them.

"Every word," came the reply. "We need to find out who these two men are and where they live. I'm sure Kheraskov will want that envelope and will want us to do whatever it takes to get it."

He took a cell phone out of his coat pocket and pushed the number 2 on his speed dial. When a voice answered, the man gave him the information on the intended quarry.

* * *

Day Six—UPI—The Dow continued its slide yesterday, falling more than three hundred points. This brings the total for the week of trading to a loss of more than two thousand points or nearly 25 percent. The NASDAQ is also down by a similar percentage. In Japan, the Nikkei has dropped 15 percent. The president's chief of staff, Anthony Rizzuto, held a brief press conference to express the president's confidence in the market despite the Dow's recent volatility. His words have done little to ease investor fears as panic is beginning to set in on Wall Street.

* * *

Robert Mills sat beside the hospital bed where Elaina Grigoriev was resting as comfortably as she could under the circumstances.

"How are you feeling?" he asked.

"It hurts a little," she answered somewhat groggily. "But the medicine they are giving me to fight the pain is helping a little, but it also makes me a little sleepy."

"The doctor says I've only got five minutes, so we need to make it count," he said. "I believe you were about to tell us the name of the man that Kheraskov was introducing to his lieutenants."

"Yes," Elaina nodded. "It sounded like he said 'Mr. Oba' or something like that."

"Did you hear this Mr. Oba speak?" Mills asked.

"No," said Elaina, shaking her head. "He did say something about this man needing an interpreter, but it was then that I was discovered."

Mills stood up from his seat. "Very well," he said as upbeat as he could. "There will be two men stationed around your room the entire time you are here. You have been checked into the hospital under the name of Deborah Woodard. Try to keep that in mind. If you can think of anything—anything at all—let one of the men know, okay? In the meantime, try to get some rest."

Elaina was asleep before he reached the door.

* * *

The KGB agent's cell phone rang as he and his partner waited outside the bank. He listened for about forty-five seconds after which he nodded in the affirmative and said yes. He closed up his phone and turned to his partner. "We have new orders. Stay here until the other man called Doug comes out. Evidently, they have uncovered some new information about one of them."

*　　*　　*

Jonathan continued on to the sixteenth floor. Since it was only about thirty minutes until the time when most people went home for the evening, things were relatively quiet. About half of the secretaries were working on their computers. All of them tried to ignore Jonathan as he walked to his office. He felt a great deal of discomfort in the solitude, primarily because he was well aware that it was of his own doing, and he wished he could go back and undo what he had caused. Shutting the door behind him, he immediately sat down at his own PC and began typing the interim report to Mark Duncan that he felt would provide enough insight as to what had transpired since their arrival, careful not to leak any of the details they had been warned not to.

Shortly after eight o'clock that evening, Jonathan finished typing the report, and after deciding that it met with his satisfaction, he e-mailed it to Mark's desk, confident that it would be available the next day. As he was leaving, he noticed the only person visible on the floor besides himself was a member of the cleaning crew who was going through the various offices and emptying out all of the trash containers.

On the ride down the elevator, he couldn't resist stopping off to check on Doug's status. Upon reaching the security glass door, he spotted Doug over in the corner of the room going over some printouts. He rapped on the door to gain the attention of one of the people inside the room. All four technicians and another member of the bank's cleaning crew looked up from what they were doing and then glanced at each other, not anticipating the appearance of a stranger at this late hour. Jonathan pointed in Doug's direction as being the person he was trying to reach. Finally, one of the technicians understood Jonathan's intent and walked over to where Doug was seated, tapped him on the shoulder, and pointed Jonathan out. Doug looked up, rose from his chair, and walked over to the glass door. Pressing a button on the nearby wall, he opened the door to greet his friend.

"How's it going?" Doug asked.

"I'm finished with the report, and it should be on Mark's computer when he turns it on in the morning," Jonathan replied. "How about you?"

"I'm just about to wrap it up myself," Doug said confidently. "I shouldn't be too much longer."

"Just don't forget you've got less than an hour, or you're buying," Jonathan grinned.

"You're pretty confident I won't be able to do it," Doug said icily.

"More and more every minute. And by the way, the clock is ticking."

"You wouldn't care to add a slice of cheesecake to the wager, would you? I noticed that there was a desert shop adjacent to the hotel."

"You're on."

"So why don't you let me get back to my job, or is this one of your stalling tactics to prevent me from winning?"

"Now, would I ever do something like that just to win a bet?" Jonathan asked, laughing.

"In a New York minute," retorted Doug. "Now let me get back to my work."

"I've got to get going anyway," said Jonathan in a more serious tone. "The FedEx office they told me about closes at nine. I'll just meet you back at the hotel. And I'll go ahead and buy the hamburgers on my way. You can just reimburse me after I win."

"In your dreams." Doug let the door close and hurried back to his desk.

After Jonathan had stepped onto the elevator, the technician closest to where the conversation had taken place walked over to Doug with a puzzled look on his face. "I thought I heard you say about twenty minutes ago that you had retrieved what you came down here for," he said.

"You know it, and I know it," Doug grinned devilishly. "But my friend doesn't have to know it, does he? This way, I get a piece of cheesecake for free out of the deal. I'll wait a few minutes to call him on his cell phone and let him know. It kinda builds up the excitement a little."

The technician couldn't help but laugh. He walked past the man cleaning out the trash receptacle as he headed back to his desk.

*   *   *

Jonathan was just about to walk into the Kinko/FedEx when his cell phone indicated that Doug was calling.

"Yes," he answered.

"It's 8:50 by my watch, and I believe it's now official," Doug's voice announced. "Just make sure you get my order right."

"I kind of suspected that I was being set up all along," said Jonathan. "That was pretty sneaky. You've been playing me like a Stradivarius."

"You know what they say, don't you? Never give a sucker an even break."

"Where are you right now?" Jonathan asked.

"I'm just getting ready to walk off the elevator, grab a taxi, and head on back to the hotel," Doug replied. "I'll be waiting long before you get here."

"Well, do I have to play twenty questions, or are you going to tell me what you found?" Jonathan asked.

"Okay, the SWIFT number is BOPIPHMM."

"Speak English please."

"It's the Bank of the Philippines. The money went to branch number 281, which is in the Makati Medical Center."

"Let me read that back to you as I write it down." Jonathan repeated the information back to Doug.

"Okay. Got it. Now all we have to do is pass this on to Mills, and our job here in New York in finished. But we're also going to need something from him that we can give to Mark. Otherwise, he's going to want us to stay up here a little longer."

Doug thought for a minute. "I think that maybe he or Greenberg are going to have to talk to him personally to let him know what's happening."

"I'll bet you're right. But as long as I can be on a flight home by day after tomorrow, that's all that matters. The package should arrive sometime tomorrow afternoon, and after that, my work is finished. It shouldn't take me more than five or six minutes here, another ten getting the hamburgers, five for the cheesecakes, plus the drive time. I should be back at the hotel in thirty or thirty-five minutes tops."

"I'll be there in about fifteen. Maybe we can catch the last half of the Astros game if they're playing tonight."

"And if it's worth watching. I'm going to call Mary and let her know when I'll be home. It should be a nice housewarming gift for her."

"I'm sure she'd love to hear from you."

"See you in a little while."

Jonathan hit the number 2 on his speed dial.

A ring later, a voice came on the other end.

"Hello."

"Hi, honey. How are you doing?"

"The girls and I are doing fine. I just wish you were here, and we were somewhere else."

"I've got some great news. Doug and I should be back day after tomorrow. Maybe we can go on our trip sooner than we thought."

"That'll be great, Jonathan."

"I love you."

"I love you too."

There was a brief pause.

"Is everything all right, Jonathan?"

"Yeah. There's a lot I can't talk about right now. But everything is going to be okay."

"I'm a little worried, Jonathan. You sound a little different."

"I'm fine—really. There's been a lot of things happening that's given me a lot to think about. I know I haven't been treating you the way I should, and I'm going to do my best to change. Okay?"

"Sure. Just be careful, okay?"

"I will. And by the way, I'm sending a FedEx package to the post office. It should get there tomorrow. Can you pick it up for me?"

"Of course."

"Thanks. I'll see you in a couple of days, okay?"

"I love you, Jonathan."

"Love you too. Bye."

* * *

"Okay. This Walker person said earlier that he was going to mail the information about where the money has been sent to his home address in the overnight mail. That means it will get there tomorrow. I want to know where he lives, and I want someone to intercept that package when it arrives. I don't care what it takes. Is that understood?"

"Yes, Comrade Kheraskov."

* * *

Walker walked out of the FedEx store, having completed his task in only a few short minutes and hailed a taxi. He was amazed how numerous they were even at this hour.

"I've got two important stops to make before I go back to my hotel," he told the driver with a grin. "First, I need you to take me where I can get some great hamburgers, and second, I need to pick up a couple of pieces of your New York cheesecake."

"I can help you on both counts," the man replied, smiling. "Hop on in."

* * *

Doug got himself comfortably established on the couch in the spacious living room area of the hotel room and turned on the TV. Changing the channel a few times, he found the Astros playing an interleague game with the Red Sox, leading comfortably six to one in the bottom of the seventh inning.

He was feeling quite satisfied over the results of the day's events, especially over the positive change that had evidently come over his friend. *Nothing like a major monetary crisis to put things in perspective, eh Jonathan?*

Just then, the hotel telephone rang. Doug picked it up.

"Yeah."

"It's me. I'll be out in front in about five minutes. Why don't you come down here and help me? These cheesecake slices are huge."

"Sure, just a second. Someone's at the door. Hold on."

Jonathan could faintly pick out Doug's footsteps as he walked across the wood floor and opened the door. "Can I help you?"

Moments later, Jonathan heard a thud as if something landed on the hard wood. Someone picked up the receiver and then the line went dead.

Jonathan was filled with a sudden sense of alarm. He redialed the hotel number repeatedly with no success. "Step on it," he told his driver. He dug out his wallet and flipped the man two twenties onto the empty seat in front of him.

The taxi arrived at the hotel, and Jonathan jumped out of the vehicle before it came to a complete stop, leaving the food in the backseat of the cab. He dashed into the building and, ignoring the elevators, jumped on to the nearby stairs, taking them three at a time until he reached the third-floor ramp. He then raced down the hallway until he reached their room. The first thing he noticed to arouse his suspicions was that the door to the room was partially open.

He tried pushing it open but found that there was evidently something obstructing it on the other side. Squeezing through the entrance, Jonathan found himself staring at the most horrific scene imaginable. Sprawled across the floor, Doug lay staring face up covered with blood.

* * *

"We are now prepared to put the second phase of the operation into effect."

"Then do it immediately."

* * *

Jonathan sat on the floor, cradling his friend's head in his lap.

"Somebody help me!" he yelled frantically. Tears streamed down his face.

Doors opened, and other guests gathered at the door to witness the gruesome sight. In the distance, the faint wail of a siren could be heard. One of the onlookers ran to call for help. The sound of the siren grew louder and then stopped. Two minutes later, a pair of EMTs appeared wheeling a gurney and immediately went to work. A few moments later, two policemen joined them.

"What happened here?" one of them asked.

"We got a request to respond to the sound of a gunshot," one of the medics answered. "And this is what we found just before you arrived. I'm afraid this one's had it, but we'll have to get him to a coroner to make it official."

"Okay," replied the officer. "Do what you need to do. We'll start questioning everyone. Who's the guy just sitting on the floor?"

"I think they must be friends or something," answered the medic. "He's pretty shook up."

Jonathan sat, rocking Doug in his arms.

"Sir, we need to talk to you," said one of the officers.

When Jonathan failed to respond, the two policemen lifted him to his feet and helped him over to the couch.

"Sir, can you tell us what happened?"

Jonathan tried to regain his composure. "I called him to say I'd be downstairs in a few minutes," he began slowly. "I wanted him to come downstairs to help me carry the food in. He said someone was knocking at the door and went to answer it. I heard a thud and then someone hung up the phone. When I got here, I came up as quickly as possible. I yelled for someone to help and then you guys showed up. I need to call someone."

He pulled out his cell phone and the business card Mills had given him. Punching the number written on the back, he waited as the phone rang.

"Mills," came the short answer.

"Doug's dead," Jonathan said mechanically. "Someone killed him."

There was silence for a brief period of time on the other end. "Is there a policeman there?" he finally asked. "If there is, I want to speak to him."

Jonathan lifted the transmitter up to the closest officer. "He wants to talk to you."

The policeman took the cell phone from Jonathan and put it to his ear.

"This is Officer Hendricks," he said.

"My name is Robert Mills. I'm the director of the Central Intelligence Agency down in Washington DC. Do whatever you want to verify my identity, but I want Mr. Walker put in protective custody until I or someone from my office gets there. I'm here in New York, and I know where he's staying. Here's my number. I'll be there in about twenty minutes. Is that understood?"

"Yes, sir."

The phone went dead, and the policeman handed the instrument back to Jonathan.

"Hey, Bill!" he yelled out.

"Yeah!"

"Get over here and call for backup to finish what you're doing! You and I've got something else we have to do."

"What's that?"

"I'll tell you when you get here."

Chapter Nine

"Now tell me again what happened," Mills demanded.

Jonathan recounted the story he had given the police without any omissions.

"But why would your friend be a target? We know it's not a coincidence that he got shot. If Kheraskov had anything to do with it, he had a specific reason. Even someone like him doesn't kill indiscriminately. Either Mr. Warner had something, or Kheraskov thought he had something."

"The SWIFT number," Jonathan said. "Doug discovered it this evening, right before nine."

"Can you give it to me?" Mills asked.

"I wrote it down, but it's already on its way back to Houston," Jonathan replied.

"Great," Mills fumed. "Is there anything else you can think of that we can use?"

Jonathan thought for a moment, then stopped short.

"Wait a minute!" he said. "There is something fishy about this whole thing. The medic said that they were responding to a report of a gunshot. I heard the whole thing. There wasn't any gunshot noise over my phone."

"What do you mean?"

"Doug and I were talking, and he said someone was knocking at the door. He excused himself and went to see who it was. He opened the door, and he said 'may I help you.' Then I heard his body hit the ground. Someone walked over to the phone and hung it up."

"What company were these medics from?" Mills asked. "Do you remember any insignia on them at all?"

"I'm sorry. Other things were on my mind—like my best friend getting murdered. Wait a minute. Now that I think about it, there was something else suspicious about those guys. They got here pretty fast—like too fast. In fact, I could hear the siren approaching, and people were just then starting to come out of their rooms."

"What are you going to do now?" Mills asked.

"I don't know," Jonathan answered dully. "We were planning on flying back to Houston day after tomorrow since Doug had retrieved the information you guys needed. Now I've got to figure out how to tell his wife he's been killed by a Russian KGB agent."

"Why don't you leave that last part out until I can confirm it?" Mills suggested. "Until then, do what you have to do in order to wrap things up. I'll have one of my men with you as a precaution until you're on the airplane although I don't think you're in any danger. I think it's only Doug they were after."

"But why?" Jonathan asked, totally exasperated.

Mills shook his head in equal bafflement. "I don't know. But I promise—we'll do our best to find out."

* * *

Day Seven—*Midday news report—The Dow Jones suspended trading for the second time in one week, continuing its downward spiral. Analysts cite a growing lack of confidence in the banking sector as more and more customers are having problems withdrawing funds from their accounts. Some are uttering the word "depression," saying it is a possibility if the market does not turn around soon.*

* * *

Jonathan decided to go into the bank although his heart was not into doing it. Still, he knew he had to retrieve his laptop and wrap up other matters in the makeshift office before heading back to Houston. *How do I tell Jamie?*

An agent from Mills's office accompanied him to the bank. He waited on a couch outside the office, stone-faced in his business suit, adding to the worries of the employees walking around him.

Gathering his belongings, Jonathan walked out in the direction of the elevator with the agent close beside him. Pushing the down button, he turned around and surveyed the surroundings one last time.

* * *

Mary heaved a small sigh again as she pulled the lawnmower out of the garage. She missed Jonathan's arms around her, and though Casey and Patty were there to provide company, it just wasn't the same. She *was* grateful that he was returning sooner than expected, although she was puzzled by his seemingly depressed voice. When she asked him if there was anything that was troubling him, he responded only by saying that he would tell her when he arrived the next day.

Mary was happy to have the two girls with her for the task of cutting the lawn. She had set a huge pitcher of cold lemonade on the lawn table in the backyard along with three tall glasses full of ice. Casey and Patty had taken seats on two of the lawn chairs in order to watch their mom pull four times on the rope before the engine sputtered into life. Mary had gone up and down the lawn two times before surrendering the job to her oldest daughter. Duplicating what her mom had done, she then passed the lawnmower to her sister. It thus became a tag team game for the three, and they were almost disappointed when the task was completed more quickly than they had anticipated.

They lounged around afterward as noon approached, discussing what they might do as a family when Jonathan arrived the next day. Mary was pleased that, due to a great deal of hard work, she would be able to report that her and Jonathan's trip would only be delayed by a couple of weeks. She told Casey and Patty that after she had finished her drink, she needed to run to the post office in order to pick up a package their dad had sent. She also promised them that, as a reward for the task they had just completed, she would stop off at their favorite Chili's restaurant and pick up three Caribbean salads topped with plenty of pineapple chunks and mandarin orange slices.

Mary completed her errands quickly, and after they had completed their meal, they finished the day with a "girls night out" watching what Patty called a series of chick flicks that lasted well into the evening. The three retired after the 10:00 p.m. news into a peaceful slumber.

* * *

When Jonathan returned to the hotel, he found that his and Doug's belongings had been packed into their luggage—courtesy of Mills's staff, he was sure. On the nearby coffee table, he found a sympathy card signed by Mills expressing his condolences over Doug's death. It did little to assuage the emptiness he felt. He decided to get to bed early since his flight was scheduled to leave shortly after seven the next morning. There would be a brief layover in Atlanta while he changed flights.

* * *

Mary found herself being shaken from her sleep with a gentle hand on her shoulder. Slowly, she opened her eyes and found Casey standing over her.

"What's the matter, honey? Is everything okay?"

"Shh!" came the reply from her daughter. "I think someone may be trying to break into the house."

"Are you sure?" Mary said, somewhat groggy. "Maybe it's Patty. She didn't eat all of her salad. Maybe she went downstairs to finish it."

"It's not Patty, Mom. I already checked. Plus Cassandra is growling like there may be someone outside."

"Okay, honey. I'll check on it just to make sure. Go on back to bed."

As Casey walked out the bedroom, Mary slipped on her bathrobe and followed her. Just as she was about to put her foot on the first step of the stairs, she froze as the faint sound of breaking glass reached her ears. *Oh my gosh! Someone* is *trying to break in!* Silently, she went back to her bed and pulled open the top drawer to her nightstand. She reached inside and pulled out the thing she loathed to even touch, her husband's 9mm pistol. Quickly, she began trying to review in her mind the three lessons Jonathan had taught her at the firing range. First, the gun is loaded and there is a bullet in the chamber. "*An empty weapon only helps the burglar.*" Second, release the safety. "*The gun will not fire until you do.*" Finding the switch on the side of the grip, she used her thumb to push the safety catch forward. Finally, "*Aim small, shoot small. Just remember, this gun is the only thing that stands between you, the girls, and the thief. He would like nothing better than to take it away from you and use it on you.*"

That thought bolstered her resolve. Mary walked back over to the bedroom door. Finding herself shaking at the thought of a possible confrontation with an unknown assailant, she decided to lie prone at the top of the nearby stairs and began to pray fervently that whoever it was would stay down below. She decided he could have anything he wanted from the downstairs area, but she would not allow him to come up. For what seemed like an eternity there was silence, and she began to believe against all hope that there was nothing. But just as she was contemplating getting up and going downstairs, she saw a shadow moving against the front door glass. Again, her heart began pounding so hard that she was sure the intruder would hear it. The outline became more visible as he approached the banister. *Aim small, shoot small.* And just as she was about to issue a warning, several things occurred almost simultaneously. The first to occur was that the upstairs hallway light was suddenly flooded with light. Mary glanced over for a split second to find Patty standing by the light switch with a totally puzzled look on her face.

"Mom, what's going on?"

When Mary looked back down, she saw the man raising his right arm. Fortunately for her, he had a slight disadvantage of having to maneuver it over the railing of the stairs; that split second probably saved her life. Instinctively, she squeezed the trigger on the gun.

The report of the weapon inside the confines of the house was deafening. Mary continued pulling on the trigger. She felt something whiz over her head. Patty and Casey started screaming, and Cassandra began barking furiously. Mary kept squeezing the trigger long after the chamber was empty, and it wasn't until then that she realized that her eyes had been closed almost from the beginning. When she dared to open them, she found herself staring at the crumpled form at the bottom of the stairs, face up.

Patty continued screaming, and above Cassandra's barking, Mary heard Casey pleading.

"Mom! Can you hear me! Oh Mom, please answer me!"

Mary slowly gathered her mental faculties. The first thing she did was to try and assure the girls that everything was okay.

"Patty! Stop screaming! Casey! It's all right! Everyone, please calm down! Get Cassandra to stop barking!"

She then began issuing instructions in rapid-fire order. "Casey, call 911, and tell them to send the police. Tell them there was an attempted robbery at our house and a gun was fired. Do you understand?"

There was a moment's pause as the barking stopped. "Yes."

"Good girl. Do it now."

Slowly, Mary rose to her feet, leaving the gun on the stairs. Working up her nerve, she descended the steps, expecting at any time that the intruder would suddenly jump up from where he lay. When she reached the bottom of the stairs, however, she realized why the man would never rise again. There were two bullet wounds clearly visible on his chest, but it was the hole where his right eye had once been which assured her of his fate. Mary covered her mouth in revulsion and fought back the sudden need to retch. She then spotted the man's weapon, still in his hand, which caused her even more fear. It became apparent to her why she had not heard the weapon being discharged. At the same time, it sent chills down her spine. A man with a silencer usually had more than just robbery as a motive for breaking into a house. Attached to the gun barrel was a large cylindrical object she recognized immediately from watching television shows with her husband.

"Mom, the police said they're coming," Casey's voice announced.

Mary had no wish for the girls to see the body. "Thanks, Casey. Why don't you and Patty wait upstairs until they get here? Okay?"

"Mom, what's happening?"

"I don't know, darling. But as soon as I find out, I'll let you know."

She had no sooner uttered the last word when a knock came at the door. "Mary! It's Larry Martin! Is everything okay in there?"

The Martins were the next-door neighbors to the Walkers. Mary stepped around the body as if it was some dangerous snake about ready to strike and opened the door. In the distance, the faint wail of a siren could be heard, growing louder by the second.

Mary opened the door and found Larry in his jeans with no shirt and holding a shotgun. He looked at her, still somewhat in a state of shock. He was about to ask her again if something was the matter when he spotted the form of the man on the floor through the crack in the door.

"Are the girls okay?" he asked immediately.

Mary nodded without speaking. It was then that Larry realized that Mary was exhibiting some slight signs of emotional shock. He had seen it before in the first of his two tours in Vietnam. No matter how tough men appeared to be, the initial taking of a life, for many, was still a traumatizing event. He had experienced it firsthand when his buddy had taken a direct hit in a mortar attack in a firefight. What was left of his body had hardly been worth the effort of putting it together again.

The reflections of red and blue lights off of the houses around them and the decibel level of the siren announced the arrival of the police car. The siren was turned off as the car pulled into the driveway. Both Mary and Larry walked out to meet the two officers as they stepped out of the vehicle. The nearest ordered them to stop.

"Sir"—directing his statement toward Larry—"would you please lower your weapon to the ground?"

Larry complied with the command immediately, laying the shotgun on the ground.

"My name is Officer Gracia. Are you Mr. Walker?"

Larry shook his head. "My name is Larry Martin. This is Mrs. Walker though. I believe Mr. Walker is out of town on a business trip."

"Mr. Martin, this is my partner, Officer Davies. We received a report of gunshots being fired at this address. Is that correct?"

"Yes."

"Were you involved in the shooting in any manner, Mr. Martin?"

"No. I heard the shots being fired and came over to investigate."

Officer Gracia glanced down at the shotgun. "Well, it appears you came prepared, Mr. Martin. However, since you were not directly involved in the shooting, I'd like to ask you to go on back home for the time being. Either I or Officer Davies will be over at some point to take your statement. You can have your shotgun back, but I'll have to remove the shells. Do you have any objections to me doing so?"

Larry shook his head.

"Thank you, Mr. Martin. We'll make sure your shells are returned to you."

Larry spoke to Mary. "If you need a place for the girls to stay, just send them over to our place. Okay?"

"Thanks, Larry," Mary answered. "I'll probably take you up on that."

Officer Davies began the task of roping off much of the front yard with yellow police tape in order to keep curious onlookers, many who had already come out of their houses, from getting too close to the crime scene. Gracia motioned Mary to go inside while he walked in behind her. He kneeled over the body to examine it and then turned to her.

"Mrs. Walker, who else is in the house with you right now?"

"My two daughters are upstairs in one of their bedrooms. They're both home from college for the summer break."

"What are their names?"

"Casey and Patty."

"Would you call up to them and let them know that I'm coming up?"

"Sure. Casey! Patty! There's a policeman coming up to meet you! Come on out in the hall and wait for him!"

Gracia grabbed the entryway rug and pulled it over the body. He then turned to his partner. "Mark, call the coroner and tell him we have a deceased out here. We need him to declare so we can get this guy out of here."

Davies nodded, and Gracia began ascending the steps. When he got to the top, he noticed the gun Mary had used and used his foot to move it out of the way. Looking at Casey and Patty, he smiled at them and did his best to lighten the situation.

"Hi, girls," he said. "Been a pretty interesting evening, hasn't it? I guess you'll have something to talk to your friends about, won't you? If you'll come over here, I just need to do a quick check around the upstairs. Okay?"

The girls nodded and complied with his request. Gracia made a speedy search of all the bedrooms and then returned to the hallway.

"When we go downstairs, I just wanted to let you know that there's a dead person at the bottom. I've covered up the body, so you don't have to look at him. When you get down there just step around him the best you can and then go wait outside the front door. Got it?"

Casey and Patty both nodded, and Gracia began leading them down the steps. Despite the gruesomeness of the situation, the girls could not keep their eyes off of the rug. When they had negotiated themselves around the body, they then did as Gracia had requested and stepped outside.

He spoke to his partner again who had returned from making his call to the coroner. "Mark, I've secured the upstairs. Would you take Casey and Patty over to the Martin house? He's offered to take them in while the investigation's going on."

He then turned his attention back to the girls. "I'm not sure how long we'll be here, but we'll try and get out of your hair just as fast as we can. Now your mom will have to come on down to the police station to make a formal statement, but we'll get her back to you just as fast as possible. Okay? Mark, I guess while you're over there, you can go ahead and take Mr. Martin's statement. When the coroner gets here, I'll take Mrs. Walker down to the station."

Davies escorted Casey and Patty next door. Gracia addressed Mary.

"Mrs. Walker, I'm sorry we're having to put you through this. I'm going to do something right now that you might think kinda strange, but it's for both of our protection. I'm going to read you your rights."

Mary, at first too numb to question the man's motives, simply nodded. Gracia pulled a card from his back pocket and began reading the words she had heard so many times before on the TV detective shows. When he had finished, he asked her, "Do you understand these rights as I have explained them to you?"

Mary said, "Yes."

"Do you wish to waive any of your rights?"

She shrugged her shoulders. "I don't have anything to hide. Ask me anything you want."

Gracia smiled. "What I want to do is just ask you a few questions so that they might stay fresh in your mind. Recount for me briefly what happened from the beginning."

Mary began her story from the time Casey woke her up until the point where he and Officer Davies pulled into the driveway.

Gracia, who had been writing her comments down on a small tablet, began asking her some questions.

"Mrs. Walker, to begin with, do you have a gun-carry permit?"

"Yes. Against my wishes, Jonathan insisted I get one at the same time he got his."

"Well, you'll be glad to know that his decision saved you a lot of grief on the matter."

"Why?" she asked. "I didn't do anything wrong. I shouldn't need a piece of paper to point out the fact that I have a right to protect my family. I would have used that gun regardless, if it meant saving our lives."

"I agree," answered Gracia. "Unfortunately, there are a number of people on the left of the gun issue that necessarily don't."

"I wonder if they might change their minds if they were in my shoes tonight," Mary said with a touch of sarcasm in her voice. "Now I'm beginning to understand more and more why Jonathan is so big on the Second Amendment issue."

"Do you remember how many shots you fired?" Gracia asked.

Mary shook her head. "I have absolutely no idea. Maybe five, maybe ten. I think the clip is supposed to hold fifteen bullets, but I'm sure it wasn't fully loaded. I just kept pulling the trigger until it stopped firing. I guess I just sort of panicked."

—

"You did what most people would do in a stressful situation," Gracia assured her. "Don't berate yourself over it. Now, I am curious. How were you positioned when you started firing the gun?"

"I was lying down at the top of the stairs," Mary answered. "Why?"

"It's probably what saved your life or, at least, from sustaining a serious wound," Gracia replied.

Mary looked at him with a quizzical look on her face.

"When I went up to get your daughters, I saw a bullet hole in the wall right where you would have been if you had been standing upright."

"I thought I heard something whiz over me after I fired that first shot."

Just then, the sound of another car pulling up into the driveway reached their ears.

"That'll either be the coroner or our sergeant," Gracia said.

As they walked out the door, a heavyset man in his sixties was emerging from the passenger side of a white vehicle with lettering on the side. Another man, much younger, stepped out from behind the wheel. Most of the first man's hair was receding, leaving a small amount on the side. He and Gracia greeted each other as if they knew one another quite well.

"You'll find him behind the front door to your left," Gracia said. "I don't think it will take you very long to call it, and I'm sure Mrs. Walker here will be glad when you can get it out of here."

"We'll put a rush on it and get him out of here ASAP." The man grinned. Mary got the distinct impression that examining a body made for a typical day in his life. *What a dreary existence.*

Just then, another patrol car pulled up. "That'll be our sergeant," Gracia said. "He'll take you back to the station and take a formal statement."

As the uniformed man approached them, Gracia made the introductions. "Mrs. Walker, this is Sgt. Tyler Haroldson. We just call him Ty down at the station. He's been with us for over thirty years, and he'll be responsible for driving you down there. So you'll be in his capable hands."

Mary realized Gracia was undertaking to relax her as much as possible and appreciated his efforts. After he had made the introductions, Gracia took Haroldson aside and spoke to him briefly in private for a few seconds.

Sergeant Haroldson spoke. "Mrs. Walker. Why don't we get in my car, and I'll take you back to headquarters. They should be able to finish up out here while we're there."

He escorted her to his vehicle and opened her door for her. After she had stepped in, he closed the door and walked around to the driver's side where he slipped behind the wheel. The drive to the police station was accomplished in almost complete silence. The officer attempted to engage her in conversation with little or no success. Her short responses to his questions demonstrated to him that she was not in a talkative disposition. Haroldson understood. It wasn't often that a person took another's life without having serious doubts afterward. When they arrived, he took Mary into a private office and invited her to have a seat on one side of the lone desk.

"Would you like to have a cup of coffee or something else to drink?" he asked. When Mary shook her head, he nodded. "The detective will be in here in a few minutes for your statement. After that we'll get you back home."

Haroldson walked out of the office, and Mary observed him through the open door speaking to a man in a business suit out in the hallway. The man nodded as if in understanding and walked into the room. Walking up to Mary, he offered his hand in greeting. "Mrs. Walker. My name is Detective Robert Gracia. I won't bother how you are doing here in the middle of the night. Suffice it to say, you've had an exciting evening."

When he saw the puzzled look on Mary's face, he chuckled. "You must have met my son tonight. I heard he got the call on the shooting incident."

Mary smiled. "You should be quite proud of him. He was very polite to me and very professional tonight."

Gracia smiled. "I'll be sure to pass your comments on to him the next time we run into each other. Now, I'm going to ask you a few questions, but before I start, do you have anything you'd like to know first?"

"Well, there is one," Mary said. "When I told your son that my two daughters were upstairs, he went up the steps with his hand on his gun like he was prepared to use it. Why?"

"Like you said a moment ago, he was being very professional," Gracia replied. "What you have to remember, Mrs. Walker, is that when a police officer arrives at the scene of a major crime, especially when it involves a shooting, he doesn't really know what to expect. For all he knows, you could have been the bad guy or, even more plausible, there could have been a confederate upstairs. He only has knowledge as to what he's been told by the dispatcher, and believe me, more people than you realize don't tell the truth. Anything else before we get started?"

"How long will this take?" she asked. "I'm tired, and I'd like to get back to my daughters."

"In all honesty, Mrs. Walker, it might take a few hours. Even when a shooting of a burglar appears as straightforward as this."

Mary could not hide her disappointment and, for a brief moment, thought she might start crying.

"Why?" she asked.

"Well, to begin with, we have to wait for the coroner to officially pronounce the guy dead. And then—"

"I don't understand that." Mary interrupted him with a touch of exasperation in her voice. "He's so clearly dead."

"We both know that," Gracia continued. "But it all has to be legal. As I was about to say, after the coroner makes the call, they have to bring the justice of the peace to do an inquest. Then they have to bring in the identification team to take pictures of the whole place, inside and out. That can take a while. Then they have to do the forensics, blood samples, and all that. Any other questions?"

Mary shook her head.

"Okay, then it's my turn."

Gracia basically made the same general inquiries that had already been asked. Occasionally, he would ask Mary to clarify a point, all the while making annotations in the notebook he had brought with him. As the session drew to a close, Gracia asked what she considered a curious question.

"Mrs. Walker, do you have any idea as to why someone would want to break into your home?"

"I'm not sure if I understand the question. I suppose he thought we had some valuables worth stealing."

"Do you?"

"Not really. I have very little jewelry, certainly not any more than my friends or neighbors, and we don't have paintings or anything valuable like that."

"One of the reasons I asked the question is that your home is basically in the middle of your subdivision, which makes a quick getaway a little more difficult for someone who might have that in mind. A common thief wants to be able to get away from the scene as quick as possible."

"You said 'one of the reasons' a few seconds ago. Did you have another?"

"Yes, I did. Did you notice anything unusual about the robber when you went downstairs?"

"You must be referring to the silencer attached to the end of his gun. Yes, I saw it."

"Then you know what it's used for. To kill without making any noise."

The statement sent more chills over Mary although she did her best to hide her fear.

"I watch movies," she said somewhat defensively.

"Then I'm sure you're aware that it's definitely not something an ordinary thief can pick up at the local Wal-Mart. Not that one can't be had for the right price, of course."

"I'm sorry," said Mary. "I'd like to be of more help if I could."

Gracia spoke again. "My son called me while you were coming over here. He said he's never seen one like it before but that it's not a homemade silencer. Which means that it was made somewhere else, probably outside this country."

"What are you trying to say?" Mary asked, a little frightened at that point. "That he was some sort of spy or something?"

"I don't know, really. But sometime in the next twenty-four hours, I'm going to have one of my people take it to the downtown Houston office of the FBI and have them take a look at it. It should be right up their alley. Maybe they can supply us with some answers."

Up to that point, adrenalin had been sustaining Mary, but all of a sudden, she found herself trying her best to stifle a yawn.

Gracia smiled. "I think we've kept you up long enough, Mrs. Walker. It's been a tough night, but I want to thank you for putting up with us this long. I'll have someone take you home. Goodnight."

Chapter Ten

When Mary arrived home, it was almost four thirty in the morning. There were no lights on at the Martin household, so she decided to let everyone sleep until later in the morning.

*   *   *

The younger Gracia brought the silencer and the weapon from the burglary into the police station for his dad to examine.

"So what do you think?" he asked. "I'm not familiar with the gun. I've also had the guys lift the man's prints and run them on the database of known felons, but it came back empty."

"Let's see what we can find on the Internet," said his dad.

The elder Gracia leaned over his computer screen and began pulling up information on pictures of handguns.

"Let's see," he said. "First of all, we both agree that the gun was not manufactured in the U.S. The man is definitely not Oriental, so I'm thinking European." He kept scrolling through various pictures and came to a sudden stop. "Well, I think we've got a hit. What do you think?" he said, spinning the monitor around for his son to look at.

"GSh-18," said the young man thoughtfully. "Made in Russia in the late '90s. Are you thinking what I'm thinking?"

"Probably KGB," answered the dad. "Jackie!" he called to his secretary. "Get me the number to the CIA in Langley, Virginia. I need to speak to someone up there about a gun."

Gracia looked at his son. "So what did you think about Mrs. Walker?"

"She doesn't have a clue. Either that or she's the best actress I've ever seen."

"I agree," nodded the dad. "You should have seen the fear in her eyes when I mentioned the purpose of what a silencer is for. Have you found out anything about her husband?"

"A little. He's some hotshot investigator for the FDIC. Evidently, when there's a big problem with a bank, the FDIC calls on him and his partner to take care of it. He's up in New York right now on some emergency assignment with one of the banks up there."

"Well then, that tears it. You know there's got to be a connection between what's going on up there and what happened down here, but I haven't got a clue as to what. We all know what's going on in the news with the banks, and I'll bet my pension there's a tie-in. I'm sending what we've got to the CIA and let them figure it out."

*   *   *

Day Seven—AP news report—*The Dow Jones has suspended trading for the 3rd time this week. Every analyst who has been interviewed agrees that there is concern in the private sector about the security of the nation's banks. One analyst, speaking on the assurance of anonymity, has gone as far to say that there is growing panic among a large number of depositors across a wide spectrum of the population. Some banks are reporting that many depositors are asking to liquidate their accounts and to close them. One bank in Sacramento, California, was forced to close yesterday afternoon because it had run out of cash in its vaults. More such incidents are anticipated.*

*   *   *

Jonathan stared out emptily of the window of the jet. The pilot had just announced to the passengers who might be interested that they were getting ready to fly over the Mississippi River. He had made the decision to call Mary at some point before he landed, and he guessed that now would be as good a time as any. Pulling his cell phone from his pocket, he punched in the speed dial number to the house. On the third ring, Mary picked the phone up.

"Hello," she said in a tired voice.

"Mary?" Jonathan asked, somewhat surprised. "It's almost 7:30. I thought for sure you'd be up by now. Is everything okay?"

"Oh, Jonathan," she said, breaking into an almost hysterical cry, "I killed a man last night."

Jonathan gripped the phone so tightly his knuckles turned white. "Mary, what happened?"

"A man broke into our house," she managed to utter between sobs. "He started to come upstairs. Patty came out of her room and turned on the lights. I just started firing. I killed him, Jonathan." Mary began crying again. "He had a silencer. The police told me that he wanted to kill us."

A jolt suddenly hit Jonathan as to the reason for the attempted robbery.

"Mary, listen to me. I want you to listen to me very carefully. Something's going on, and I don't know what it is. That package I sent you in the mail—they killed Doug for it."

There was silence over the phone.

"Doug's dead?" She started sobbing again. "Why?"

"I just told you. There's information in that package that they want. They killed Doug for it, and they were ready to kill you too."

In a desperate voice, Mary asked, "You keep saying they. Who're they?"

"I'll tell you later. Where are the girls?"

"Next door over at the Martins," she answered, blubbering again. "Why?"

"Go get them. I want you all to pack some clothing, enough for a short trip. After you do that, get into the car and get away from the house. Then call me back on my cell phone in a couple of hours. I'll let you know what to do then."

"Why are you—what's happening, Jonathan?"

"Just please trust me on this. Okay? Doug discovered something, and they killed him for it. I put the information in the package that I sent you, and that's why they broke into the house—to get it. They would have killed you for it, maybe even the girls too. You're not safe in the house."

"Has anybody told Jamie?"

"Probably not. I'll go and see her after I get in. When you call back, I'll have a better idea about where I want you to go. You said that you thought you heard a car squealing outside right after the shooting."

"Yes. Why?"

"The guy you killed may have had a confederate. If that's the case, they may try again."

"What's going on, Jonathan? Why is this happening to us?"

"Please don't ask me a lot of questions. Okay? I've got some thinking to do."

"Where are you right now?"

"We're about thirty minutes out from Houston. What did you do with the package I sent you?"

"It's on the desk in your study. Why don't I just come get you and bring it to you?"

"Because they might come after me next, and I don't want you or the girls anywhere close to me if they try. Do you understand?"

"Yes."

"Call me back in about two hours."

It wasn't until after the plane landed that Jonathan realized that he was without transportation and was therefore forced to hire a taxi to drive him home. When they arrived at the house, Jonathan paid the driver and stepped out. Surveying the outside, he noticed the crime scene tape had not yet been removed, indicating the police had not finished with their work. He lifted the part of the material covering the sidewalk and ducked under it. Walking up to the front door, he fished his keys out of his pocket, unlocked it, and stepped inside. His first discovery was the most gruesome. On the bottom step was a huge red spot that covered almost the entire carpet area of the first step. In addition, there were a number of splashes of fresh blood on the wall. It gave him no small satisfaction that the enemy had been thwarted from achieving his goals.

Jonathan took the stairs two at a time and first retrieved the fateful package from his desk. Next, he went to their bedroom and emptied his suitcase of his dirty clothes, replacing them with a fresh set of new ones. Looking over the room, he left and proceeded out to his car. Inside, he sat for a minute, knowing what he had to do next. The trip over to Doug and Jamie's house was agonizing. He parked the car, slowly made the walk up to the front door, and rang the bell. Jamie answered a few seconds later.

"Hi, Jonathan," she said, smiling and looking over his shoulder. "Where's Doug?"

Jonathan's silence and expression told her everything. Jamie stared at him for a moment in total disbelief before shaking her head.

"Oh please, God, no."

Jonathan watched as Jamie burst into tears and sank to her knees. He could do little else other than stand in his place as she wept uncontrollably. Finally he put his hands on her shoulders and gently lifted her to her feet. He then led her into the house where he sat her down on the living room sofa. For several minutes, he let her grieve before speaking.

"I'm so sorry, Jamie. I just wish there was something I could say or do to make things better, but I know there isn't."

"How did it happen?" she dully asked after a long pause.

"He was murdered," Jonathan said quietly. "Someone shot him in our hotel room."

"Who?"

"They don't know yet. They're still working on it. But it's probably the same people who tried to kill Mary last night."

"What?" Jamie asked incredulously, looking up at him.

"Someone broke into our house last night, probably intending to kill Mary."

"Is she okay?" For the time being, Jamie forgot about her own situation.

"She's all right physically, but emotionally she's a little messed up. She shot and killed the guy when he tried to come up the stairs."

"But why would anyone want to kill Mary?" Jamie asked, totally perplexed. "You're not making any sense. She wouldn't hurt a flea."

"It's my fault." Jonathan grimaced. "There's something going on with some of the banks up in New York. You've probably heard about it in the news. Doug discovered what happened with the money that was taken and got killed for it. I sent the information in an envelope to Mary, and they found out about it. Now I have to get Mary and the girls out of town until this whole thing blows over. I also have a bone or two to pick with someone. I'll be gone for a few days, but when I get back, I'll tell you everything. Okay?"

Jamie looked at Jonathan briefly before giving him a big hug.

"Please be careful," she pleaded, trying to hold back her tears. "And don't do anything foolish. I've lost my husband. I don't want to lose his best friend too."

Jonathan smiled and walked out to his car, formulating his plan as he went. Not waiting for Mary, he called her on her cell phone.

"Jonathan, where are you?" she asked.

"I'm just leaving Jamie's," he answered. "Where are you three right now?"

"Just driving around the city. I was going to call you in a few minutes. Is Jamie okay?"

"Not really. How would you feel if someone just told you out of the blue that I had just been murdered?"

Silence.

"Mary, I want you to listen to me very carefully and do exactly as I tell you. Okay?"

"If you say so."

"Good. To start with, I'm going to give you instructions on how to get out of town without being followed, but when I tell you, I just want you to answer yes. They may be somehow tapped into your phone right now. Do you understand?"

"Yes, but Jonathan, who are these people?"

"All I can say at this point is that they'll stop at nothing to get what they want. They've already murdered Doug, and they were going to do the same to you and the girls. Got it?"

"Yes."

"Okay, to begin with, remember where my parents used to own that eight acres?"

"Yes. Of course, off of—"

"Stop. Remember what I said, only answer yes if you know what I'm talking about."

"Okay."

"Stop by the nearest rental car place and pick one up. You with me?"

"Yes."

"After you do that, call me back."

"Okay."

Twenty minutes later, she was on the line again.

"What do I do now?"

"Head toward the property with Casey driving the other car right behind you. Remember how narrow the roads are, especially where the bridge goes, don't you?"

"Yes."

"Call me right before you get there."

It took over an hour before she reestablished contact. "I'm almost there," she said.

"Stop your car right after you get over one of them. Have Casey stop on the bridge, get out, throw the keys into the creek, and get into your car."

Mary drove her car to the other side of the bridge and stopped. Bewildered, Casey stopped behind her mom on the narrow span. Mary rolled down her window and motioned her eldest to come join them. Taking the keys, she hurled them into the water.

"It's done. Now what do I do."

"Stay out of towns. Keep to the back roads for a while. You've got a little drive ahead of you, so keep that in mind. I know this will sound strange, but I want you to go to that place we stopped at about thirty-two years ago. Remember?"

"Yes, of course."

"I've got to go somewhere for a couple of days. After I've finished with what I need to do, I'll come get you."

"But Jonathan—"

"Trust me, Mary, please. I'll explain everything when I see you."

There was a brief pause. "I love you."

"I love you too, honey. Bye."

Jonathan disconnected the phone just as the boarding for his flight was being announced.

*   *   *

Kheraskov paced about his study like a caged animal. "So what you're telling me is that my agent gets himself killed by the woman he's supposed to eliminate, and then she turns around and gives his partner the slip, all within twelve hours. Idiots!" he muttered under his breath. "Have they found Obah yet?" he demanded.

"He landed in New York six hours after he left here, and we're sure he's still there. If we have to, we'll search every hotel in New York, we'll find him," the aide said confidently.

"Get me on the next flight to New York," Kheraskov demanded. "I want to be there when he's found. What about the other one?"

"He's still in a coma although the signs are that he's coming out of it. I think they probably gave him a little too much of the drug, but they said that after it has worn off, he should survive."

"Keep me informed," said Kheraskov. "He may be our last source of information."

*　　*　　*

Jonathan settled comfortably into his seat on the Boeing 747. He was quite worn-out, having been on the go since early this morning. His anger toward the KGB knew no bounds. He had just successfully changed planes for the second time, but to ensure that nothing could go wrong, he elected to wait a full hour until his flight was in the air. He punched in the new number off of the back of the card that Mills had given him. Mills answered almost immediately.

"Is this Jonathan?" he asked. "Where are you?"

"Let's just say that I'm on my way to take care of some unfinished business," Jonathan replied coolly.

"You need to come in," said Mills. "We can give you protection."

"Oh yeah, right," answered Jonathan with derision in his voice. "The way you protected Doug, Elaina, and my wife?"

"Your wife?" asked Mills, in a puzzled tone. "What about her?"

"Oh, didn't anybody bother to tell you?" replied Jonathan, his voice dripping with sarcasm. "Someone broke into our house last night and tried to kill her and my two daughters."

"But they're all right," said Mills.

"No thanks to you people. She had to kill someone for the first time in her life, and so she's having a little bit of a hard time dealing with it."

"Please, Jonathan, don't do anything dumb," said Mills, frustrated. "I'll send some people over to your house and pick them up."

"Oh, we're way past that," said Jonathan, getting even testier. "I've sent them into hiding myself, and neither you nor the KGB are going to know where. If you want to protect someone, why don't you help Doug's wife and try keeping her alive. I had to give her the good news this morning."

"Please Jonathan, come on in," Mills pleaded. "You don't know who you're dealing with."

"Oh, I think I know exactly who I'm dealing with—some nut job in the KGB who, according to what you've told me, wants to take Russia back to the

Stone Age. Now don't worry. I sent you the information that Doug was killed for by overnight mail. You should get it sometime tomorrow morning. Then you'll know where the money got wire transferred to. By that time, I should be well out of your reach."

"Is there anything I can do to change your mind?" Mills asked.

"What if you promise me you'll let me tag along when you go after the money trail," replied Jonathan evenly.

"You know we can't let you do that," said Mills, totally frustrated.

"That's what I thought you'd say," Jonathan answered. "Good-bye." He disconnected the phone and pressed the button above him to call a stewardess.

When one came, he asked her, "What time do we get into Manila?"

"Around nine thirty in the morning," she answered with a smile. "Is there anything we can get for you when we arrive?"

"No, really. It's just that I'm really tired, but I want to try and plan it so that I get about seven hours of sleep and wake up a little bit before we get there."

"Well, let's see," she said thoughtfully. "It's about three hours from Guam to Manila. We have a thirty-minute layover while we're there. So if I were to wake you up, say half an hour before we land, then you need to go to sleep in about, oh I'd say two hours. If you need to stay awake until then, you can walk around the cabin, or I can get you some coffee if it'll help any."

"I'll take you up on the coffee. And I'll take a walk around the cabin while you get it."

"How do you like yours?" she asked.

"One cream, no sugar," Jonathan replied. "Thanks."

"No problem," she smiled. "I'll be right back.

Jonathan struggled to stay awake, even with the coffee, for the next two hours and was grateful when his stewardess walked up and told him it was time to go to sleep. She reached above him to the overhead compartment and handed him a small pillow that he gladly accepted. He was asleep within thirty seconds of putting his head on the pillow.

*   *   *

"We've got to find him," Mills said, "before he gets himself killed too. He was on the phone long enough to get a fix on his position. Find out where. Also, I want someone down in the mailroom tomorrow morning to get that package the moment it arrives. I'm sure Walker will be on the other end of it."

*   *   *

8:00 p.m. local—Danil Petrova of Russia's Department of Finance landed in New York to discuss his country's upcoming grain purchase for the approaching winter. His entourage picked him up and got him into his limousine outside the terminal.

"Well?" asked Kheraskov.

"Obah is dead," the driver informed him. "His body was discovered yesterday morning by the hotel's cleaning crew when a bad odor started coming from his room. He evidently committed suicide in some type of Japanese ritual."

"What about all the men who helped him?"

"All murdered," came the reply. "Every one in the same hotel in different rooms with a bullet in the back of his head."

"And our friend?"

"Better news on that front. He came out of his coma last night. When we showed him who we had as hostage, he gave us the information we needed."

"And?"

"It went to a bank in the Philippines."

"The person who received the wire must have sent it to someone else," Kheraskov said. "That much money would stand out too much. I could probably buy the Philippines for what we are talking about."

Chapter Eleven

9:30 a.m. (Manila)—Jonathan walked out of the Ninoy Aquino airport in Manila still not feeling totally refreshed. He attributed it to the fact that his body was still on New York time, half a world away. Before leaving, he stopped an airport official about the way to get to the Makati Medical Center and was told the best way, though slightly more expensive, was to take a taxi as it was several miles away. He also learned that everyone accepted both American dollars and the local currency of pesos.

There were a number of taxis outside although it took a considerable amount of time to escape the terminal area due to a huge crowd waiting outside.

"Is there some important person arriving?" Jonathan asked the driver.

"No," the man grinned. "Not really. Here in the Philippines, leaving and coming home is a family event. In some cases, dozens of relatives will come to say hello or good-bye."

"And what are those funny-looking cars over there?" he asked, pointing to a colorful number of vehicles lining the streets.

"They are called jeepneys," he answered proudly. "When the Americans left after World War II, they left all of the jeeps behind and donated them to the Filipino people. The Americans have always been a good friend to us."

Jonathan smiled. "It's good to be appreciated sometimes by the rest of the world," he commented. "It doesn't happen very often."

The drive proved to be interesting though uneventful. After the driver had entered the main thoroughfare, Jonathan was surprised by the mass of traffic that was on it. He was also slightly amused by the fact that even though there were lines clearly marking the delineation of lanes on the highway, there was a total disregard for them. There were only cars, jeepneys, trucks, buses, and other various modes of transportation, all jockeying for position in an attempt to gain an extra foot of space even though no one appeared to be in a particular hurry.

As they approached his destination, the driver asked Jonathan where in the medical center he wanted to be taken.

"The Metropolitan Bank" was the reply.

His driver nodded and began maneuvering his taxi over toward the curb. Jonathan paid him, throwing in a generous tip, and thanked him for the ride before exiting the vehicle.

Taking a deep breath, Jonathan walked into the spacious building and surveyed his surroundings. It was quite crowded with bank customers. One wall was taken up by tellers conducting business with the customers on the other side of the counter. Except for a single hallway, which Jonathan guessed led to the bank vault and the other auxiliary offices, the remaining walls contained a series of small offices, most of which had gentlemen in business suits sitting behind large desks. Half of them had people across the desk obviously discussing bank business. Outside each office sat a secretary in front of a PC, and there were a number of couches spaced throughout the spacious area. The men and women who sat on the sofas were all well dressed, which contrasted significantly to people he had observed outside the building. His assessment was that the bank catered to a distinct class of clientele and that there was a great disparity between the haves and the have-nots.

Jonathan walked over to a desk that the person behind it, he hoped, could point him to the person that could provide him with answers to his questions. The woman behind the desk looked up at him and, immediately assessing that he was American, addressed him in English.

"May I help you?" she asked.

"Yes," he replied. "I need to speak to someone about a wire transfer."

"If you go down that hall," she replied, "it is the first office on the right."

"Thank you."

Walking down the hall, Jonathan felt slightly conspicuous. He was a full head taller than virtually every person around him, and he got several glances, he was sure, because of it. The single exception appeared to be an American or European, he was not sure which, who was sitting on one of the couches, apparently waiting to see a loan officer.

Jonathan stepped into the office and found two men—one a Filipino and the other probably of Japanese descent—busily at work, obviously preparing a series of wire transfers that were in a wire basket on a nearby counter. The Filipino man looked up and smiled.

"May I help you?" he asked.

"Yes, you can," Jonathan replied. "First of all, are you the only ones at this bank authorized to accept wire transfers?"

"Yes, we are. Is there a problem you experienced?"

"Yes, there is. It concerns a wire transfer that came to this location about eight or nine days ago I believe."

"Well, it might take a little time to look for it. This is a very busy bank, and we send out and receive many wire transfers every day. If you could fill out one of our forms, we could research it for you."

"Oh, I don't think it will take you too long to find this one," Jonathan said evenly. "All you have to do is look for the amount—about three-and-a-half trillion dollars."

The smile disappeared from the man's face.

"You must be mistaken, sir. This bank is not set up to handle transactions that large."

Jonathan pulled out a piece of paper from his pocket and jabbed his index finger on it. "Nevertheless, this paper says you did. A wire transfer for that amount came to this bank location eight days ago. Here is the bank routing number it went to, and that's you."

The man looked at the slip of paper but remained silent.

"Maybe it would be better," Jonathan remarked casually, "if I spoke to someone else in the bank—like your supervisor. There's already been one murder and two other attempted ones over this transaction. And I'm sure we're also talking about wire fraud."

The man glanced down at the paper and looked back up at Jonathan. He no longer seemed as cordial as before. The Japanese man joined them at the counter.

"I could not help but overhear your conversation," he said. "If you will be so good as to wait here, I will get the bank officer in charge, and you can discuss it directly with him."

"Thank you, I'd appreciate that," Jonathan nodded.

The Japanese man walked out of the office. Jonathan observed him through the glass window, but instead of going to another bank employee, he approached a security guard and began speaking to him in earnest while gesturing animatedly and pointing in Jonathan's direction. Jonathan then saw the security guard reach for his gun and begin to walk in his direction. At once concerned, he stood up and began looking around for an exit when, all of a sudden, an explosion rocked the center of the lobby outside, and while he observed no visible signs of damage, a great deal of smoke began filling the area. The sound of bullets firing in the air followed, and panic ensued among the people as they scrambled for the exits. For a moment, Jonathan was at a loss of what to do when a firm hand grabbed him.

"Quick," a voice said. "Come with me."

Jonathan followed, somewhat dazed from what was transpiring around him. When he glanced up, he found himself staring at the same man who had been seen sitting on the couch earlier. The man led him into the midst of the terrified crowd, allowing themselves to blend in among the people as they rushed outside.

Once out on the sidewalk, Jonathan turned to his rescuer.

"Okay, who are you, and what just happened in there?"

"The name's Andrew Green. CIA. You can call me Andy. And what happened in there is what we call in our business a small diversion. Come with me to my car. It's parked not too far from here. I'll explain everything when we get there."

"But who told you I'd be here?" Jonathan demanded.

"Mills notified me this morning. He said you'd be flying into Manila. Evidently, he was able to get a GPS fix on you when he spoke to you last night, and his people were able to determine what flight you were on. It wasn't difficult, just time consuming."

They got into Green's car.

"I guess I'll have to remember never to use my phone again if I'm concerned about being bugged," said Jonathan sarcastically. "And do you mind telling me what your 'little diversion' was?"

Green pulled out a small rectangular object from his coat pocket. "I just press this button, slip it under the sofa where I was sitting, walk away, and seven seconds later, *poof!* I call it my American Express card," he grinned. "I never leave home without a couple of them on me."

"Well, I appreciate you bailing me out back there," Jonathan said. "My goose would have been cooked otherwise."

"Seriously," Green said, "the best thing you can do for yourself is to get back on that plane and fly back to where you came from."

"Well, if that's all you have to say, then I will thank you again for getting me out of there, but I'm not leaving until I get what I came for."

"Mills said you'd probably say that," Green replied. "So all I can say is just stay close to me, and we'll decide what to do next."

"All I know is that I spooked that Japanese guy when I mentioned the wire transfer," Jonathan said.

"If that's the case, we'll go around to the underground parking lot and wait where the employees park and see what happens," nodded Green. He started the car and drove off.

"So how do you seem to know so much about this place?" commented Jonathan with a hint of suspicion in his voice.

"We've had these guys under our radar for quite some time," said Green. "We've known for some time that a terrorist group named Abu Sayyaf has been using this bank to conduct their wire transfers of money. They're the most radical of the Muslim groups operating in the Philippines. They obtain most of their money through the kidnappings of Western businessmen and wealthy Filipinos, which they then turn around and use to conduct their terrorist operations. The Philippine military does their best to go after them, but they're pretty slippery. And they don't mind dying for what they believe in—which is to kill as many infidels, which are us, as possible. For them, it's some kind of wacky command they believe comes from Allah to do so. They think it's their one-way ticket to get to their seventy-two virgins when they get to heaven."

"I hope they all turn out to be a bunch of ninety-year-old Catholic nuns," Jonathan growled.

Green grinned. He liked Walker despite the man's stubbornness—maybe because of it. Mills had told him about what he had learned and about the focus Jonathan had about him, Doug's death, and the attempt on his wife's life. Green decided it made for a deadly combination for someone. He just hoped it would not be for Jonathan himself.

The CIA man parked his car so that they had an unobstructed view of where the bank's employees who used their own transportation would come out.

They had scarcely settled into their place when they spotted the Japanese man hurrying out the door and into his own car. He took off as if in a great haste to get somewhere.

Green followed, allowing plenty of space to develop between the two vehicles, but not so much that he lost sight of his quarry. He obviously had had much experience in tailing someone in as heavy a traffic as they were in. Their target seemed to have a specific goal in his mind as he pointed his car in a westerly direction, eventually leaving the city behind him.

"I know where he's heading," said Green grimly after they had driven for about twenty minutes.

"Where?" asked Jonathan.

"Corregidor," answered his host. "The KGB sometimes use it as a rendezvous spot whenever they want to meet someone and make sure that they're not being followed. The only way you can get to the place is by boat. It's an island that the Americans used in World War II to try and hold off the Japanese from getting to Manila Bay. They held off for as long as they could, but they were finally forced to surrender."

"Yeah, I'm familiar with the story," Jonathan said. "If you're in the corps at A&M, you learn they held one of the most famous musters ever during the siege."

The drive took almost two hours. Green's assessment as to their destination turned out to be correct. From a distance, they could observe the Japanese man park his vehicle in a visitor's parking space and hurry off to purchase a ticket for the next ride that would ferry him over to the island. Green waited until he was out of sight before parking some distance away.

—

"We'll wait until his boat is well on its way. It'll take him about seventy-five minutes to make the trip. We'll get something that's a little faster and do an end run on him," said the CIA agent. "We'll be waiting on him when he arrives."

Green hurried down to the water where a group of vessels were moored. Nearby were a small number of men lounging around, evidently waiting to be hired out as personal tour guides. Walker observed him as he and some of the drivers seemed to be engaged in haggling over the cost of the trip. Soon, a price was evidently reached at to everyone's satisfaction and Green quickly returned with a smile on his face.

"They do love to bargain over here," he remarked, grinning. "It's almost a sign of weakness if you don't. Keep that in mind if you ever decide to come back for a visit." He pointed to the ferry a couple of hundred yards away. "The man we're chasing will be on that boat with a bunch of tourists. It takes about seventy-five minutes by ferry. We'll get there in less than an hour."

Walker and Green waited for nearly thirty minutes before a group of about twenty people including some young children tramped out of the nearby building and down to the large ferry where they loaded on to the vessel. Green waited until he judged the passengers to be out of range of recognizing them, and then he and Walker hurried down to their private transportation. Giving the ferry a wide berth, they circled around to a spot where they could land unobserved. Once they had landed, Green took a hundred-dollar bill out of his pocket and tore it in half. He gave one piece to their pilot and told him to wait there. "You'll get the other half if you're here when we get back."

The man grinned and propped his feet up on the wheel of the boat. "For one hundred dollars, I would be willing to drag my boat upon dry land if that is your wish."

"Good, but that won't be necessary," the CIA man responded in a serious tone. "We shouldn't be gone too long."

"I hope you're up for a little exercise," Green said to Jonathan as they walked away. "The first place they'll stop will be the Malinta Tunnel, which is where the Americans hunkered down when the Japanese were bombing them," Green said. "The tunnel is a great place for a rendezvous. Or they may be meeting on top of the island where the big guns were placed. If that's the case, we'll have to hightail it back down to the dock and hire a jeepney to take us up to the top of the island. Just be prepared to move quickly. Got it?"

Jonathan nodded, and they began a brisk walk up the dirt road. Reaching a certain spot that Green judged they could view both the dock and the entrance to the Malinta Tunnel, they stopped behind some bushes. From their vantage point they could look in one direction over the clear blue water. Green pointed to a small dot in the ocean. "That's the ferry," he said. "It'll be here in about ten minutes. They'll board that tour bus down there which will then drive them a few hundred yards over to the Malinta tunnel. The tourists unload and their tour guide shows them around for about twenty minutes. Then they all get back on the bus and head toward the top part of the island. There are a few points of interest along the way like the barracks that were basically destroyed in the bombings but no place to really walk around until they get to the top."

Jonathan watched as the dot on the water grew rapidly larger until he could make out the people on the ferry. The boat's pilot maneuvered it easily on to the dock where a guide was prepared to receive them. He quickly led them on to the bus. Jonathan and Green easily spotted the Japanese man as the latter was one of the first to exit the ferry and, unlike his fellow tourists, did not seem very happy.

The tour guide was the last to board their transportation, and Jonathan could barely discern him picking up what he guessed was a microphone in order to provide information about the upcoming tour. The short trip to their initial stop took less than thirty seconds where everybody got off and made their way into the tunnel, which appeared to be about twenty feet wide. The guide made a count of them as they disembarked.

"The tunnel goes all the way through that mountain—about six hundred feet," Green said. "Inside the main tunnel, there are a bunch of side arteries that branch off where the Americans kept their supplies and ammo. They also housed their wounded in there during the war."

As Green had indicated earlier, the tour inside lasted about twenty minutes. The guide repeated his head count as everyone boarded the bus but seemed puzzled as if there was a discrepancy in the number who got on. Jonathan immediately noticed that the Japanese man was not among the ones who got reboarded.

The tour guide waited for some time for the missing person to appear and then gave a shrug of his shoulders, evidently surmising that anyone left behind could be picked up on the way back. Walker and Green waited until the bus had gone completely out of sight before emerging from their hiding places. As they reached a point about fifty feet from the entrance, Green stopped and pulled out a weapon from his coat.

"Okay," he said. "I don't want any arguments on this. Stay here out of sight behind some of these bushes. I'm going to walk to the other end of the tunnel and start working my way back while I look inside some of the branches inside. If the Japanese man comes out before I do, it means he somehow gave me the slip. Wait for at least ten minutes until after he leaves. When it's safe to do so, then you can come in and look for me if you want. I don't think he's got a gun, but you never know. It's my guess that he's inside one of the branches meeting with some KGB agents."

He had barely uttered his last sentence when two men with looks of satisfaction on their faces emerged from the tunnel entrance. Jonathan momentarily froze although Green did not. He shoved Jonathan, who was on his right side, hard to the ground and dove to his left all in the same motion. At the same time, both men in front of them pulled out firearms of their own and commenced shooting. A fierce but short gun battle ensued. From where he had landed on the ground, Jonathan looked up and saw that both of the enemy agents had fallen down, and when they did not get up, he slowly rose to his feet.

"You got both of them," he said with a great deal of satisfaction. But when there was no response from Green, he turned his head to discover the CIA agent still lay on the ground, barely moving. Jonathan rushed over to the man's side and turned him gently over on his back. A bullet wound in the left right upper part of Green's chest was clearly visible, and he was evidently in considerable pain.

"Listen to me carefully," Green whispered. "I'll be okay. Drag all three of us into the brush, and hide our bodies. I can call my people from my cell phone, and they'll send someone out here to help me. When they find these two, you can't afford to be around and get caught by the police. You'll never be able to get out of the Philippines. The Japanese guy is probably inside the tunnel, dead. Which means that those guys killed him for whatever he knew. They're both KGB. You can take his place on the ferry to get off the island. Take the keys out of my pocket. When you get back to the mainland, take my car and drive it back to the airport. Catch the next flight out of here, today if possible. I'll call Mills and let him know what happened."

Jonathan looked around momentarily before acting on Green's instructions. He dragged the three men into some nearby brush, making Green as comfortable as he could. Almost as an afterthought, he began rifling through the clothing of the KGB agents, taking all of the money in their possession and transferring it into that of his own. He also took the other half of the hundred-dollar bill from Green's pocket as the CIA agent had lapsed into unconsciousness. Jonathan checked to make sure he was still breathing. In one of the KGB men's pockets he discovered a piece of paper that he unfolded. Inside he found a series of a combination of seven letters—IRVTUS3N on one line and a nine-digit number, 8328161938, below it. He recognized the lettering as being similar to the SWIFT number that had led him to Manila, and in all likelihood, this was the checking account number to go along with it. Excited over the discovery, he pocketed the paper and ran into the tunnel. In the first branch toward the back, where the lighting was dim, he discovered the body of the Japanese man lying facedown with a bullet in his brains. Jonathan conjectured that after he had contacted the KGB with his information, they had lured him to the rendezvous spot. He guessed they had probably promised him safe passage out of the country and then carried out their gruesome execution once he had arrived and given them what they wanted. Again, he went through the man's pockets and removed anything of value.

Deciding nothing more could be done, Jonathan elected to forego waiting for the tour bus to make its return and instead hiked back down to the private craft. Along the way, he called Mills as he was concerned over Green's safety that he might not wake up from his injury. Not wishing to get into a lengthy discussion, he gave Mills a quick assessment of the situation and hung up. He then hurried down to the water where he found their pilot comfortably napping where they had left him.

"Here is the other half of the hundred-dollar bill," Jonathan said, handing it to him. "My friend has one more thing to do. He said he'll catch the ferry to get back."

The pilot happily nodded since it meant he could then take the rest of the day off, and they were soon heading back to the mainland. Back in the parking lot, Jonathan got behind the wheel of the CIA man's car and took stock of how much he had in his possession. Fortunately, there were only dollars and pesos he had to contend with, and when he had added it all up and mentally converted the pesos to dollars, he figured he had roughly $6,000 on him. More than enough, he conjectured, to return to the States without using his credit card.

It took him a while to determine the best method of getting back to the airport before remembering what Green had told him about the Filipinos. *They love to barter around here.* Jonathan drove around until he found some men walking along a main thoroughfare.

"Excuse me," he yelled out the passenger side window. "I'm lost. Is there anyone here who would be willing to drive me to the airport? I'll pay him fifty dollars."

The question immediately galvanized three of the men to rush his vehicle and offer to take him. After some haggling among themselves, one got in the car, exchanging places with Jonathan in order to sit behind the wheel. The drive took about an hour, but when they arrived, the Filipino man received a totally unexpected surprise. Jonathan not only gave him the money but took the keys out of the ignition and handed them over to him.

"Thank you so much for your help," he said. "Keep the car as a gift for your family."

The man's joy knew no bounds, and after thanking his obviously wealthy benefactor profusely, he proudly drove off in his new possession. Jonathan smiled and walked into the terminal. He quickly purchased a ticket although it necessitated a considerable wait, since the flight was not scheduled to depart until almost eight o'clock that evening.

Just before boarding his flight, he was alarmed to notice on a nearby television monitor a newscaster speaking in his native tongue of Tagalog. But it was the pictures that concerned him the most. TV crews had evidently convened on Corregidor and were filming the apparent discovery of several dead bodies and one other injured person on the island. Three of the men, according to the report, had firearms on their persons. Jonathan was particularly glad to see that Green, although on a stretcher, appeared to be doing well. He smiled at the thought of what the agent might be telling the authorities when he was able to talk.

Chapter Twelve

Day Eight, 9:00 a.m. (New York)—In a hastily convened meeting by the board of directors of the New York Stock Exchange, all trading has been suspended until further notice as there appears to be no end in sight to the market's free fall. The NASDAQ quickly followed suit. The Fed has instructed the Department of the Treasury to print an additional $500 billion and dispense it to any bank that is experiencing a shortage of funds due to a high level of demand from depositors. In a related story, there are a number of accounts where fights are breaking out inside banks between depositors who are attempting to liquidate their accounts.

The stewardess informed Jonathan shortly after taking off from Manila that the flight to Los Angeles would take about eleven hours, depending on any tailwinds they might be able to take advantage of. Doing some quick mental calculations, he figured that, taking the time zone changes into account, they would be landing at almost the same time of day as when they had left. Feeling exhausted from what had transpired during the day, he asked the stewardess to wake him about halfway between Guam and Hawaii. She handed him a pillow from one of the overhead compartments, and within minutes, he was sound asleep. He was only vaguely aware of the brief stopover in Guam.

When the stewardess woke him, Jonathan only felt slightly refreshed but somewhat bolstered by the fact that he would soon be able to join Mary and the girls in Cloudcroft, New Mexico, the place where they had spent their honeymoon almost thirty-two years ago. He decided to call her before calling Mills. Plugging his cell phone into the jack on his armrest, he hit the speed dial for Mary's phone. It rang once, but it was not answered by Mary or the girls but by a deep masculine voice.

"Mr. Walker," he said. "I've been expecting your call for some time now."

"Who is this?" Jonathan demanded.

"My name is Dimitri Kheraskov," he replied. "Perhaps you have heard of me."

"Yeah, I know who you are."

"Then you know that I am not someone to be trifled with. You should tell your wife to be more careful when she uses her credit cards. Bad things can sometimes happen."

Jonathan swore silently to himself for not warning Mary about how they could be traced.

"You have something I want," Kheraskov continued.

"Oh, you mean like the location of about three-and-a-half trillion dollars, don't you?"

"Something like that."

"So what do you propose?"

"A simple trade. The location of the money for your family. Tell me where it is, and I'll let them go."

"I don't think so," Jonathan replied with a sneer in his voice. "You think I don't know I'd be signing their death warrants if I did. Let me talk to my wife. Now."

"And why should I do that, Mr. Walker?"

"Because if I can't, I can only assume that you have killed them already, and there would be no reason to continue this conversation. And then I could start making plans on how to find and kill you."

A new voice came on the phone after a brief pause.

"Jonathan?"

"Are you and the girls okay?"

"We're doing as well as can be expected. They have us cooped up in some hotel room, but they haven't bothered us."

"How many nights did we spend in Cloudcroft?" Jonathan asked her.

"Four," came the quick, quizzical reply. "Why did you want to know that?"

"I just wanted to make sure I wasn't listening to some type of recording device."

"Jonathan, what do these—"

The voice disappeared as the phone apparently changed hands again.

"I think that is enough to satisfy you for the time being, Mr. Walker," Kheraskov said. "I will be waiting for you when you return from your trip."

The connection ended abruptly, and Jonathan found himself staring into empty space. Figuring he had about three hours until they landed in Hawaii, he began wracking his brain for ideas on how to extricate his family from their current predicament. As a realist, he knew their lives hung precariously in the balance. Kheraskov, he knew, could not allow them to live and identify him. They were nothing but pawns to him, in a chess game, to be discarded if need be. It was incumbent on him, therefore, to stay at least two moves ahead of the KGB man and to keep Mills from entering the picture, at least at this time.

Slowly, he began to formulate a plan in his mind, the first step being one of disinformation. First, he called the CIA switchboard in Langley, and when an operator answered, he spoke in a terse manner to the recipient.

"Listen very closely as I will not be repeating myself. My name is Jonathan Walker, and this message is for Director Mills. I am on my way back from the Philippines and will be ready to meet someone in Los Angeles if he wants. Tell him I have the information he needs and not to bother calling me back because I won't answer. Good-bye."

Disconnecting, he put his phone back into his pocket.

When the plane landed in Hawaii, instead of remaining on board, Jonathan disembarked and made his way to an Aero Mexico counter where he purchased a ticket, with cash, to Mexico City. As luck would have it, a plane for his new destination was scheduled to depart only thirty minutes after the flight he had originally been on was to leave. Jonathan's hope was that by the time Mills realized he was not on the plane when it landed on LAX, he would already have reached his new destination and disappeared into Mexico's capital. Once the new flight was airborne, he asked a stewardess for a list of all the ports of entry between Mexico and the United States. With the aid of two other flight attendants, he determined the one that best suited his needs was an entry called Antelope Wells, the westernmost point of entry into New Mexico. Thanking them for their assistance, he next called New Mexico's state capital in Santa Fe and obtained the next vital piece of information in his plan. With only a short hour until the flight was due to land in Mexico City, Jonathan then began formulating his plan and how to implement it.

As soon as the plane landed, he was prepared with suitcase in hand and was the first to disembark. He quickly made his way through Customs and out to the front of the terminal where he grabbed a taxi and ordered the driver to take him to a clothing store.

The first thing Jonathan wanted to do was to transform himself from a traveler into a hiker. Inside the store, there was no need to ditch a suitcase, since he had left it back in Manila. His first order of business was to purchase a knapsack. He next purchased a pair of blue jeans, a sturdy pair of tennis shoes, and two pairs of athletic socks in the hope of preventing blisters on his feet. Ducking into a changing room, he put on his new clothes. He then had his driver take him to a food store where he bought several candy bars and a number of fresh fruits that he loaded into his knapsack. Stepping back into the taxi, he surprised his driver by telling him that he wished to be taken to the New Mexico border crossing at Antelope Wells.

"Señor, that is much too far to take you. It would be at least seven hours plus the drive back."

"I'll pay you $500 in cash plus your meals and gas up there and back if you can drive me up there today," Jonathan said, holding up a wad of bills.

The other man paused only briefly. That much money was more than he would normally bring home in two months.

"My taxi is at your disposal," he said with a grin.

Jonathan returned the smile while reaching into his pocket. "Here is one hundred dollars to show good faith on my part," he said, handing the man five twenties. "You'll get the rest when we reach our destination. Agreed?"

"*Sí.*"

"Then let's get going."

The car took off from the curb, and Jonathan settled himself comfortably into his seat. "I'm going to try and get some sleep," he told the man in front of him. "Just wake me up if you need gas or want something to eat."

When Jonathan was aroused from his slumber, he found himself sitting at a gas station. The driver was just in the process of putting the gas nozzle into the car, so he took the opportunity to step out of the taxi and stretch his legs. His companion looked up from what he was doing.

"Are you hungry, señor?" he asked.

"I could use something to eat, I suppose," Jonathan answered, "as long as it's not too spicy."

"Tacos?"

"Sounds good. And if they have beef fajitas, I'll take some of those too. Will twenty dollars be enough?"

"Yes."

The man disappeared into a building adjacent to the gas station, and when he came out a few minutes later, he held a small bag in his hand. Jonathan had already finished topping off the tank and had replaced the gas nozzle back into the dispenser. He handed his driver a fifty-dollar bill to cover the cost of the gasoline, taking the bag of food in exchange. While the driver took care of the bill, Jonathan climbed back into the taxi and began unwrapping the foil around the food. He was working on his second taco by the time his companion returned, this time with two large bottles of Coke. When he stepped into the car, Jonathan kept two of the fajitas for himself and handed the bag's remaining contents forward, taking one of the drinks.

"We are about three hours away from Antelope Wells, señor. We should get there at about seven o'clock this evening. Are you aware that the gates close at four?"

"No problem," Jonathan answered. "I've got a friend who'll be picking me up tomorrow morning."

The rest of the ride was completed in relative silence. When they arrived at the Antelope Wells port of entry, Jonathan thanked the man and paid him the balance of what he owed, throwing in a generous gift for his efforts. As the taxi drove off, he took stock of his surroundings. The landscape was basically barren, and there was no fence that needed to be negotiated. Jonathan picked up his knapsack and began walking north along the two-lane paved road that led into New Mexico. For a while, he walked in the dirt along the shoulder. He hoped that by the time he was discovered, he could pass as someone who had been spending some time in the outdoors. Nighttime came quickly, and he found himself staring at a totally black sky filled with stars more numerous than he had ever imagined. *I've got to show Mary and the girls this*, he thought to himself. *I didn't know how much the city lights blocked out.*

When morning finally arrived, Jonathan felt sure that he could easily pass himself off as a tired hiker—which was exactly how he felt. He had no idea how far he had walked but guessed he had put at least seven or eight miles between him and the place where he had entered New Mexico. He hoped it wouldn't be too long before someone would come along and offer him a ride. Shortly before nine o'clock, he finally spotted a car approaching, the glint of the eastern sun bouncing off it as it neared. The first thing that struck Jonathan was how wide it appeared. As it came more into focus, he recognized it as a Humvee painted in camouflage with two men sitting inside. The vehicle slowed as it approached. The men, both clearly of Mexican descent, wore uniforms identifying themselves as Border Patrol agents.

"You look stranded," the man in the passenger seat said. His name tag had the name Compeon on it.

"Maybe a little," Jonathan replied, hoping he could pull off a decent acting performance. "I was originally supposed to meet a friend of mine back at the border crossing, but he called me on my cell phone late yesterday and informed me he got held up back in Houston and couldn't make it. I decided to start hitchhiking. My family's waiting for me in Cloudcroft. My wife let me do a little hiking beforehand because I've always wanted to. She and our two girls had no desire to do any serious walking, so I'm out here by myself. If you want, I can show you my passport, and I'll be more than happy to let you go though my stuff. I can promise you that I don't have a nuclear weapon or anything," he said, smiling.

The driver of the Humvee got out of the vehicle and walked around to where Jonathan was standing. He, like his partner, looked as though he spent a lot of time in a weight room and, despite a broad grin on his face, came across as a no-nonsense type of individual.

"Well, Jose, what do you think?" The name on his tag read Ramos. "He doesn't look much like an illegal, and he definitely doesn't sound foreign. I guess if he can show me a valid U.S. passport and let me look inside his bag, then I'll believe him."

Jonathan opened his bag, pulled out his passport, and handed both to the agent. He glanced briefly at the passport, looked inside the bag, and then returned them to their owner.

"I suppose you check out." The agent grinned. "We can give you a lift as far as Deming. After that, you're on your own."

"That'll be great," Jonathan replied. "If I can find a car rental place, then I'll be in good shape."

"Then hop on in," the man named Compeon motioned to the backseat.

During the drive, Jonathan had a chance to talk to the patrolmen about their take on the rampant illegals pouring across the border. He learned that they were just as disgusted as he was about the seeming indifference by the people in Washington. When he tried to find out why there was no apparent sympathy on their part toward their fellow countrymen, he got back a sharp rebuke from Ramos.

"We are not Mexicans, Mr. Walker," Compeon said firmly. "We are not even Mexican-Americans. We are American citizens who happen to be of Mexican descent. We came across legally and took the necessary steps to learn English and become American citizens. I'm proud of where I came from but prouder of what I am now. My allegiance is to the United States."

"Why aren't you running for Congress?" Jonathan asked him. "I'll donate right now. I'll even be your campaign manager."

The agents laughed. "We'll keep you in mind, Mr. Walker," Ramos said.

The drive up to Deming took about an hour. Jonathan thanked the two men for their assistance and hopped out of the car in front of a Hertz rental car agency. Jonathan quickly paid for a one-way car rental, bought a map, and headed for Albuquerque. On the way out of town, he determined that the trip to Albuquerque would take about four hours. Along the way, he ran through in his mind what he was going to say in his letter to the FBI agent in charge of the office. Jonathan knew one thing; there was no way he could allow Kheraskov access to the money he had pilfered from the banks. The effect on the U.S. economy would be devastating, not to mention the horrible havoc the KGB could bring upon the world.

When he reached his destination, Jonathan located a Kinko's office outlet, parked the car, and walked into the store. Sitting down at an empty computer screen, he quickly typed the letter and printed it out. Purchasing an envelope, he folded the sheet of paper and placed it inside. Lastly, he jumped into the car and made his way downtown to the federal courthouse. After parking his car, Jonathan strode purposefully into the building and found the FBI's offices on the marquee. Standing in front of the door, he took a deep breath and stepped inside. A secretary sat behind a desk, busily typing on the computer in front of her. She looked up and smiled.

"May I help you?" she asked.

"I have a letter for your office director. It's from some guy who paid me twenty dollars to bring it to you," Jonathan answered. "He said it's from someone named Robert Mills in Washington DC, and it deals with some guy by the name of Jonathan Walker. I believe it's urgent."

The secretary took the envelope and glanced at the letter.

"Just a minute," she said in a concerned voice. "I'll be right back."

Thirty seconds later, a man burst into the reception area only to find it empty. "What did he look like?" he yelled back to the secretary. The woman quickly joined him and gave a brief description of Walker.

"Great!" Albert Druce, manager of the local FBI office, muttered. "That *was* Walker. Get ahold of Robert Mills at the CIA in DC. Let him know that Walker's in our area and ask him what he wants us to do. And fax him this letter immediately—top priority."

Druce looked down at the paper again. *In less than forty-eight hours, I will have to turn over to Kheraskov the information he wants to get to the money if I have a chance of saving my family. You have that much time to do what you need to recover the money. The* SWIFT *number is IRVTUS3N.*

*　　*　　*

Robert Mills sat at his desk staring at the paper in front of him while his deputy stood in front of him.

"What should we do?" the man asked.

"First of all, we find out where the money is using the SWIFT code," Mills replied. "Walker at least gave us that much of a chance. If we have to, we then send an army of agents to that bank and take it over if necessary. After that"—he shrugged in frustration—"we try to find out how we can help him find his family. Kheraskov must have them. And if he could find them, then we should be able to do the same. I'm just afraid he's going to get himself killed first."

Chapter Thirteen

Jonathan bolted from the FBI office the moment the secretary left her desk and made his way as quickly as he could back to his car without drawing attention to himself. Getting into his rental vehicle, he made his way on to Interstate 10 in an easterly direction. Within an hour, he was entering El Paso, Texas. *So far, so good.* His first order of business was to stop at a hardware store where he made some quick purchases. His next was to find a gun shop. His reasoning was that it might be easier to purchase a weapon in his home state as he did not know what New Mexico's gun laws were and did not want to spend an inordinate amount of time filling out paperwork in order for them to conduct a background check and then possibly have to wait for several days for them to conduct it. It took longer than he wished to locate one, but he was glad that once he located a weapons dealer, his license to carry a firearm helped him in obtaining one. When he walked out, he was now in possession of a .22 revolver, a clip that would hold fifteen bullets, and a box of additional shells. Outside of the store, he made one more phone call.

"Hello," came a voice on the other end.

"Let me speak to my wife," said Jonathan.

The phone was handed to Mary. "Jonathan?"

"How are you and the girls?"

"We're doing fine. But that man is pretty agitated."

"Let me talk to him. And don't worry. I'll be seeing you in less than twenty-four hours." Jonathan was not as confident as he sounded.

Kheraskov's voice came back on the line. "Yes."

"I just crossed the border," Jonathan lied. "I have to get a ride into a nearby town so that I can rent a car. I'll call you sometime tonight."

He immediately disconnected the phone and put it in his pocket.

On the other end, Kheraskov stared at his phone and then looked up at Mary. It was not often he did not feel totally in control of his circumstances, but Walker was making him feel just that.

"Your husband makes a very interesting adversary, Mrs. Walker," he remarked.

"That's because he's the best at what he does," Mary replied defensively. "He and his friend Doug, before you killed him."

Kheraskov just stared at her and walked away.

*   *   *

Jonathan drove as quickly as he could to his next destination. Continuing on to I-10, he briefly headed north back into New Mexico, and when he reached Las Cruces, he turned east on to Highway Eighty-two. After almost three hours of driving made longer by the curvy road (it seemed), he finally reached the small town of Artesia where he turned south on to Highway 285. Late in the afternoon, he finally reached Carlsbad, the town made famous because of its proximity to Carlsbad Caverns National Park. The entrance to the park brought back many fond memories to him. On several occasions, his grandparents had taken his family to the enormous caves, and he had never ceased to be amazed at the way the entrance into the caverns opened up for view as the visitor approached on foot. He had taken Mary there for their honeymoon. But this time, it was different. The chances were that, this time tomorrow, they would all leave together, or none of them would leave alive. It was a terrible burden that Jonathan placed upon himself but one he knew he had to accept. He had flown F-4s over North Vietnam in the war and had dropped plenty of ordnance that he knew would result in the deaths of innocent civilians, but the thought of bringing his own loved ones directly into harm's way was something hard to deal with. *Still, I don't have any other options. If I don't succeed, they'll be killed anyway.*

Jonathan knew he had one advantage. He had some idea about where he would insist for the meeting to take place. He knew Carlsbad National Park had only one entrance into it, and he would therefore be able to guarantee, within some limits, his control over it.

He entered the park and made his way up the winding road until he came to the first place where visitors could pull off to the side and park a car. On one side of the road was the hillside, dotted with shrubs and trees, mostly pine. On the other, where his car sat, was a steep ravine that dropped steeply over two hundred feet into a narrow valley. Jonathan stepped out of the car, opened the truck, and removed the items he had recently purchased. Surveying his options, he picked up his cell phone and made one more call as he walked across the road and made his way up the hillside.

Kheraskov answered immediately.

"I'll be waiting for you at the first visitor viewpoint inside the entrance to Carlsbad National Park," Jonathan said. "It's about two miles inside the park entrance. I'm assuming you're not too far away. Be there at 6:00 a.m. tomorrow, but don't show up early. Come alone and bring my family with you, or you'll never see me."

"I'll bring them in a separate car, but I will not let them remain. You will be able to see from your location that they are safe."

"Keep them close by. I'll want to talk to them before we finalize our little business transaction."

"I don't think I trust you, Mr. Walker," Kheraskov said dryly.

"Ditto," replied Jonathan. "And by the way, don't bother calling me when you reach our rendezvous point. I won't have any of your men trying to locate me by my voice."

"How will I find you then?" Kheraskov asked.

"I'll find you," Jonathan answered as he hung up. Surveying his surroundings, he found a suitable spot and placed the equipment on his person under a tree.

*   *   *

Just off the eastern coast of the United States, in a bank not unlike the one in Manila, an interesting scenario was being played out. In teams of two, forty men wearing dark sunglasses slowly trickled into the spacious lobby and made their way into various locations throughout the bank. If anyone made notice, they did not seem overly concerned. The bank was typically used by people outside the country to hide their money in offshore accounts. What was not typical was what happened within the span of the next few moments. Verifying that everyone was in place, a man tapped a button on his lapel and gave the command to execute their tasks. At the same time, each team strategically placed themselves in various offices throughout the building to ensure that no warnings could go out. Several men dressed in white hazmat clothing suddenly appeared outside the bank's doors to seal off any further entrance into the bank. Those people who were hoping to go in and conduct their banking business were told that several envelopes containing a white powdery substance had been received by the bank and there was a strong suspicion that they might contain anthrax.

Inside the bank, they were dressed quite differently. Every man produced a weapon, and suddenly, the demeanor inside changed. Several women screamed until one of the men, brandishing a gun, walked into the middle of the lobby and fired two shots into the air, warning everyone to be silent and assuring them that no one would be hurt if they followed the instructions they were given. Upstairs, twelve men entered the bank's executive floor and forced their way into the CEO's office over the strong objections of his secretary. When told he could either accompany his captors to the bank's wire transfer department willingly or be dragged there, he chose the former. When they reached the wire transfer office in the building's basement, they found a differently dressed man awaiting them in addition to the bank's chief operating officer. He was sitting over a computer terminal and studying the screen in front of him to determine what transactions had taken place in the account in the last few days. Calling the team leader over, he pointed something out.

"Well, well, well," the team leader commented. "What have we here? Print that out," he said. "I'm sure Mills will be interested in that tidbit of information."

"We're not sure who in the bank was involved, but you two will arrange for all of the money that is in these accounts," the man said, pointing to a scrap of paper, "and transfer it to these seven accounts."

Pulling a cell phone from his coat pocket, he asked the person on the other end if the seven people were ready to receive the wire transfer. When the answer came back in the affirmative, he turned to the operations officer, "Here is the first one. You will transfer this amount to this bank's general account."

Six more times the same operation took place. At each location, the money was returned in the exact amount as was taken from it nine days previously, including money that would have been earned on any interest-bearing accounts. Under joint orders from the Federal Reserve chairman's office and the comptroller of the currency, all overdraft fees were waived.

After the last of the transactions had been completed, the bank's employees were herded into the spacious safety deposit box area and locked in. Before leaving, one of the gunmen slid a cell phone under the metal, smiled, and said thank you. He then walked out to the bank's lobby and thanked all of the customers for their cooperation. As quickly as they had appeared, the forty-one men vanished, leaving the people in the bank bewildered but happy to be unharmed.

*   *   *

Jonathan tried as best he could to find a comfortable place on the ledge, which would be both out of sight from the road where he was parked and as safe as possible since he did not want to roll over during the night and fall into the ravine. He knew the temperature would fall enough to make it uncomfortable without suitable protection, which was why he had taken the precaution of buying sweatpants and a heavy overcoat.

He had a specific plan in mind for his meeting with Kheraskov in the morning but rehearsed the scenario in his mind over and over, trying to account for anything that his adversary might try to spring on him. One of the strengths he and Doug had brought with them to the FDIC was their meticulous attention to detail, which had served them well over the years. Laying his head down, he drifted off to sleep.

*   *   *

During the night, seven groups of people worked around the clock to ensure that every account was restored to the condition they had been in prior to the theft of almost two weeks ago.

*   *   *

Day Nine—*As reported yesterday, all trading of the stock markets have been temporarily suspended. In other related news, President Collins met with Fed chairman Andrew Greenberg yesterday evening over the crisis in the stock market. Although details of the meeting were not disclosed, it is reported that the president will have some positive information regarding the banks, which have also recently been under intense scrutiny. As soon as further information is made known, it will be released.*

*   *   *

Despite the clothing, the night was anything but comfortable. Several times, Jonathan awoke to find himself rolling dangerously close to the edge of his sleeping area. At around 4:00 a.m. he decided to remain awake, feeling convinced the adrenalin coursing through his body would overcome any feelings of fatigue. At around 5:00 a.m. he could hear a number of cars passing by on their way to the cave entrance. It was the visitor's opportunity to witness the return of the Mexican free-tailed bats back into their sleeping quarters deep within the recesses of the caverns after their nightly excursion of foraging for their food, which consisted of flying insects. At 5:30 a.m. he made his way to a location along the edge where he could observe Kheraskov's arrival without being seen. At 6:05 a.m. two cars slowly pulled into the observation area. To Jonathan's satisfaction, the people in the cars appeared to have their attention almost totally focused on the wooded area on the other side of the road. The driver in the rear car stopped and stepped out of the vehicle. Opening the rear door, he evidently gave some instructions to the people inside. In a matter of seconds, Mary stepped out followed by both daughters. Aside from the fact that none of them were smiling, they all appeared to be in excellent health. When the man felt there had been sufficient time for Jonathan to see them, he ordered the three back into the car.

Jonathan then turned his attention to the lead car. Inside, there appeared to be only a single figure who he guessed was Kheraskov. Jonathan witnessed the man bend over slightly and then open the door and step out. It was at the same time Kheraskov bent over, Jonathan thought he caught a slight movement at the rear of the car out of the corner of his eye although he failed to see anything out of the ordinary. He was forced to admit that Kheraskov cut an imposing figure despite wearing only typical clothing. Before exposing himself from behind the elements, Jonathan scanned the entire area to ensure as much as possible that there was no likelihood that he was walking into a trap. When he turned his attention back to Kheraskov, he noticed one more thing—Kheraskov's lips were moving slightly as if he was speaking to someone. It was at that point that he realized there was someone hiding in the trunk, which altered his plans slightly. When Kheraskov leaned against the vehicle facing the hillside, Jonathan crept over the edge and snuck up to the car unobserved.

Kheraskov opened all the doors to the car. Then he spoke out in a booming voice, "Mr. Walker, I assume you can hear me. As you can see, I am alone and unarmed."

Jonathan stood up from behind the other side of the vehicle, his gun leveled at the man across the hood of the car. "I'm right behind you, and I have a gun pointed at your head, so don't make any sudden moves. At this distance, it would be difficult to miss."

Kheraskov turned around slowly and smiled. "You are Mr. Walker, I presume," he said.

"Mr. Kheraskov," Jonathan nodded.

"It is unfortunate you and I are not on the same side," Kheraskov said. "You would have made a strong asset to my team."

"Yeah, but then again I don't normally associate with murderers, bank robbers, and kidnappers," Jonathan replied evenly.

"So what do you propose we do now?" the KGB man asked, unruffled by the affront.

"Well, to begin with, we need to make a short trip," Jonathan said. "You've got a nice car, Mr. Kheraskov. Is it a rental or one of yours? Not that it really matters, I suppose. I'm sure you'll be able to buy a new one with three-and-a-half trillion dollars. By the way, I'm glad to see that you've left the keys in the ignition. And now, why don't you step a few feet away from it so that I can check it out."

Since the ground consisted primarily of small rocks, Walker had no problem in spotting one that suited his purpose. Picking it up, he carried it around the driver's door, maintaining a constant eye on Kheraskov. With one eye on his adversary, he leaned in and turned on the ignition. Quickly, he jammed the rock between the accelerator and the floorboard. Reaching inside with his right foot, he placed it on the brake pedal, threw the car into forward gear, and stepped back. The rear wheels spun briefly in the gravel, and then the vehicle lurched forward over the concrete parking barrier before disappearing into the ravine.

Jonathan turned his attention back toward Kheraskov. "I hope you didn't lose anything of value in there," he said sarcastically.

Kheraskov remained silent.

Jonathan motioned to the Russian with his gun. "Start walking," he said. "We're going to take a little trip to the other side of the road."

Kheraskov shrugged his shoulders and began walking with Jonathan about five or six paces behind him.

Kheraskov turned his head as they walked. "I assume you do not like me, Mr. Walker," he said.

"Oh, I'd say we're way past that point," Jonathan replied evenly. "I stopped disliking you right up to the point when I discovered you were the one who broke into my home and tried to kill my family." After they had crossed the road and gone a few feet, Walker said, "Stop!"

"Surely you do not intend to kill me, Mr. Walker," replied Kheraskov as he turned around. "You need me to get your family back."

All of a sudden, there was a loud report from the gun in Jonathan's hand. Kheraskov screamed in agony, falling to the ground and clutching his left knee. Blood oozed from the joint mixed with the white of the cartilage. With equal indifference, he walked up to the Russian and pointed the weapon at the other knee and squeezed the gun again. Kheraskov screamed once more.

"I will make you two promises," Jonathan said, nonchalantly. "The first is I will not kill you. The second is if you don't answer the questions I'm going to ask you to my satisfaction, I will begin inflicting so much pain on your miserable body, you'll wish I had."

Kheraskov had never experienced fear before, but when he saw the steely look in Jonathan's eyes, he became genuinely afraid.

Walker bent over to the Russian and spoke, "I'm told that in order for the threat of force to be effective, the person upon whom the threat is made has to believe that the threat will be carried out. But then again, I'm sure you of all people know that."

Placing his foot on the KGB man's left knee, he pressed down. Kheraskov screamed again.

"Rest assured that I will use whatever means necessary to obtain the information I desire. There are a number of other joints in your body I have access to. As it is now, you'll probably be walking with a cane or sitting in a wheelchair for the rest of your life. Do I make myself clear?"

Jonathan pressed down again.

"Yes!" Kheraskov screamed again.

"Good," said Jonathan. "You know, I've heard it said that most bullies are basically cowards. We'll soon see. You see, Mr. Kheraskov, you made a grievous error in kidnapping my wife and daughters. You made me make a choice between my family and what was best for my country. But because I couldn't allow you to have access to all that money, I was quite prepared to allow you to kill them in order to prevent you from getting the bank account that you wanted. There's no way I could allow you to get control of that much money, no matter what you might have done to them. Which makes it easier to do to you what I have in mind. I turned the information over to the CIA yesterday, and I'm sure that they're taking whatever steps necessary to have it returned. Now, where is my family being held?"

"The La Quinta Inn," Kheraskov moaned in pain.

"What room?"

"One hundred forty-two."

"How many men are there?"

"Two."

"And finally, one last question for the time being. What have you got planned for tomorrow? And be careful how you answer it. Your immediate medical attention will depend on it."

*   *   *

Jonathan left Kheraskov firmly tied to a tree with a wad of cloth stuck inside his mouth to prevent the Russian from calling out for help in his absence.

"You'd better hope I'm successful," were his parting comments. "If I'm not, you will die a very lonely, painful death right here."

*   *   *

Jonathan pulled up to the hotel at about 6:30 a.m. and walked quietly up to room 142. There, he stationed himself outside the door. Fortunately, no other guests of the hotel came out of their rooms during the next half hour while he waited for the occupants inside to make a move. It came shortly before 7:00 a.m. when he heard the sound of a male voice, definitely in a foreign tongue, approaching the door from the other side. Jonathan swung the gun around, grasping it by the barrel. The door opened, and a man started to step outside when Walker pivoted around, bringing the butt of the weapon down hard on top of the man's head, causing him to crumple to the ground in a heap. Jonathan switched the gun handle back around and stepped over the form blocking his path. The commotion caused the other man in the room who was sitting on the lone bed and whose back was initially facing him to spin around. Seeing his companion lying on the floor, he started to reach inside his jacket.

Jonathan said in a cold tone, "Just give me an excuse, comrade. At this distance, I can hardly miss. Get on the floor, face down and hands out where I can see them. And slide your gun over to me."

Slowly, the man did as he was ordered.

"Mary!" he called out. "Can you hear me?"

The bathroom door slowly opened.

"Jonathan?" came a woman's voice.

"Come on out slowly. I want all three of you to crawl over the bed and wait outside the door."

As Mary started walking past her husband, he reached behind her neck and brought her to him, passionately kissing her. Mary looked briefly surprised before grabbing him and returning the embrace. Their daughters looked at each other and grinned.

After Jonathan and Mary separated, Jonathan handed her his cell phone. "Find Robert Mills on my phone and call him. Tell him where you are. I bet there'll be a team of agents out here in less than an hour. After that, I want you to take my gun and keep this guy covered until they arrive. You won't have any reservations about shooting him if he tries to escape, will you? After all, they were probably going to kill you and the girls."

Mary looked grimly down at the man lying prone on the floor. "I don't think I'll have a problem if it comes to that," she answered, cocking the weapon. "I'm a redhead, and I've already killed one Russian in the last week. I don't think one more will make any difference."

Jonathan grinned. "You know, sometimes I love it when you get mad."

*   *   *

"You're doing good, so far," Jonathan said as he walked up to Kheraskov. "Just answer me one more question, and after we verify that you've told me the truth, I'll call for an ambulance."

The KGB man looked up as Jonathan removed the cloth from his mouth.

"Where is he?"

Chapter Fourteen

A helicopter landed inside the parking lot of the La Quinta Inn less than forty minutes after Jonathan called Mills, and even though local police officials had arrived minutes earlier, the display of certain badges to them left little doubt as to who was in charge. Mary turned over the gun in her possession, much to the relief of her prisoner.

"We have one dead man, you say you're guarding some Russian KGB guy, and that's all you can tell me?" he asked with incredulity. "Mr. Walker hit the man so hard that he died a few minutes ago from a subdural hematoma."

"I'm sorry, but I really don't feel particularly sorry. Those two were going to kill us if Jonathan hadn't done what he did. And I honestly don't know where he went," she told Albert Druce. "His instructions were to tell you to wait for a short period of time and that you would be getting a phone call from some man named Robert Mills as to where you could pick him up. He said he had some unfinished business with a man nearby."

Druce threw up his hands in exasperation and looked at Mary. "I might as well buy you a cup of coffee while we wait for your husband's call," he sighed.

It was a typically warm June morning in Houston, Texas, with humidity already approaching 80 percent. Since it was 6:00 a.m. on Sunday, most people were just getting up in preparation to attend church, sleeping in, or arriving at home from a night's carousing at nearby drinking establishments. The police presence was always heaviest during this time in an attempt to minimize accidents caused by inebriated drivers. On the 610 East Loop at the Highway 225 exit, things were also normal although several changes had taken place there during the night as well as several other key locations throughout the vast city.

"The target vehicle is now on 610 East traveling south over the Houston Ship Channel. To reaffirm, the target vehicle is an 18-wheeler tanker truck with markings of Shell on the tanker portion. Louisiana license number KGT 2475."

"That is affirmative. How sure are we about the intel on these guys?"

"Very. It supposedly has come directly from Mills. Confidence remains high. Both places the truck has passed have shown a huge spike on the counters."

"How about the occupants?"

"It's confirmed that both men are of Middle Eastern descent. The man in the passenger side appears to be reading something. He's bobbing his head up and down like one of those bobble head toys, so he's probably reading his Koran. I hope he chokes on it, if that's the case."

"He'll never get the chance. Delta Three, do you copy?"

"Affirmative, Base."

"Target vehicle should be approaching your location in about five minutes. Have you been copying the transmissions regarding the description?"

"Affirmative."

"He'll be in the right-hand lane to take your exit. When he does, we'll pass the ball on to Delta One for a final go or no go."

"I copy."

*   *   *

Inside the cab of the semi, two men were making final preparations.

"Will you be ready to arm the weapon when we get to our destination?" the driver asked the other.

"Yes. Allah be praised. We will be glorified at that moment. We will cut off the head of the Satan United States, and the snake will begin to die. Allah be praised. We will wreak vengeance upon it for what they have done to our people, and we shall feel nothing. Allah be praised."

"Here is the exit we need to take," said the driver. "Allah be praised."

*   *   *

"Delta One, this is Delta Three. Target has turned on to Highway 225 and is heading your way. You should have a visual in about sixty seconds. The counter read another spike when he passed our location. Confidence still remains high."

"Roger that, Delta Three."

"Good hunting."

"Base, this is Delta One. Are we a go or no go?"

"It is affirmed that you are a go, Delta One. It comes from Mills. How long will it take to deliver the package?"

"Judging from the distance from here to the highway, not long. I'd guess no more than two seconds."

"Make sure he passes you before you deliver the package. We don't know if the bomb is already armed or not, and I don't want to give them any more warning than we have to. How accurate can you be?"

"Are you kidding? With this technology, I could put one through the driver's window if it's rolled down. Speaking of which, the target is now visible and will be within range in a few seconds. I have now painted it."

"Good luck."

The men inside the truck were right about one thing—they never felt a thing.

*   *   *

Day Ten—*The New York Stock Exchange reopened today amidst a great deal of trepidation as to what effect the previous day's layoff might have. There was apparently some good news from the banking sector which occurred overnight, which the banks were unwilling to discuss until now. Apparently, one of the large computer hardware companies that provides equipment to many of the large banks was discovered to have some type of virus in them, causing major problems with their accounts. The source of the dilemma was finally discovered and has now been corrected. In other national news, a tanker truck owned by Shell Oil Corporation apparently ignited for reasons unknown at this time on one of the main arteries leading to its refinery in Pasadena, Texas. For many, the explosion reveals a growing concern of what might happen in the nation's energy capital if a major disaster were to occur there, where not only oil is refined but also where the majority of the country's petrochemical industries are located. Two men, the driver and his companion, were apparently killed in the blast, which was fortunately limited to the front portion of the truck. An unconfirmed report says that a single eyewitness claims seeing a streak of smoke coming from across the highway and hitting the vehicle. As a precaution, the area was cordoned off for some time while Hazmat personnel were quickly dispatched to deal with any unforeseen circumstances.*

*   *   *

The ring came from the cell phone inside the pocket of Jonathan Walker's jacket. He removed it and listened to the voice on the other end.

"Good. We'll be waiting for someone at the first turnaround inside Carlsbad National Park," he replied. "I suggest you make arrangements for a medical team who can treat gunshot wounds."

An ambulance and a limousine arrived within fifteen minutes of Jonathan disconnecting.

A medic took a quick look at the damage Jonathan had inflicted. "It looks like he may be going into shock," he commented. "Plus, when he recovers, he'll probably never walk again unless it's with considerable pain."

"As it should be," Walker commented indifferently.

He walked over to the waiting limousine where a man with dark sunglasses was leaning up against it. "Mr. Mills would like to talk to you personally," he said somewhat dryly.

"I'm sure it's not of a celebratory nature," Jonathan answered.

"I would assume that's a pretty safe bet," came the reply.

"What about my family?" Jonathan asked.

"They are being escorted back to your home as we speak," the agent assured him. "I also think Mills and Chairman Greenberg has some information that they want to share with you."

* * *

In a small neighborhood just on the Maryland side of the Potomac River, a man stepped out of his front door and walked over to his car. He observed a man and a woman jogging nearby as he stepped into his vehicle. As he reached over to start the car, he heard a tap on his window. Looking up, he found himself staring into the barrel of a .38 revolver with a silencer attached to it. The man behind the gun was grinning evilly. On the other side of the car, the woman he had observed moments earlier jogging was also aiming another gun at his head.

"Would you mind stepping out of your car for a moment?" the man asked.

Outside of the car, the man was forced none too politely against the hood by the male jogger. The woman placed herself about ten feet away, never taking her eyes off her quarry.

"Your boss wishes to speak to you," said the CIA man, handing a cell phone over to him.

* * *

Jonathan stepped off the private jet and looked at his welcoming party. Foremost among them was Doug Warner, with Alan Greenberg and Robert Mills close behind. Jonathan walked up to them and paused briefly before giving Doug a firm handshake followed by a fierce hug.

"I knew you wouldn't stop looking for me," said Doug.

"I'm sure Mr. Mills was just as suspicious," answered Jonathan. "There were no gunshots that I heard over the phone, and the other hotel occupants didn't hear anything either, although I suppose they could have used a silencer. But the real kicker was how quickly the ambulance showed up at the scene and how it somehow just magically disappeared with your 'body.'"

"So how did you find out where they put me?" asked Doug.

"You might say I just put a little fear of God into Kheraskov. When he realized I was prepared to be just as cruel as he is, he folded like a cheap suit. He gave up your location, and Mills here did the rest."

"Yeah, once Mr. Walker here gave me the location, it didn't take much to step in and subdue them. There were only two guys watching. Although I can't say I agree much with your methodology, we got what we needed."

"Jamie says you're dead meat when you two meet again," Doug grinned. "For convincing her I was dead. But afterward, she says she'll give you a great big hug."

"I can live with that," Jonathan smiled.

* * *

A group of five men, three in military uniform, strode down the long hallway inside the White House. When they reached the door leading into the Oval Office, the ranking officer called them to a halt. "You are hereby relieved of your post, corporal," he spoke in precise terminology.

The corporal looked surprised momentarily but obeyed the order from his superior.

"We shouldn't be in there for more than five minutes, Sergeant," Mills said. "He needn't go very far." Opening the door with authority, he walked in with Greenberg close behind.

Collins and Anthony Rizzuto, who was sitting opposite, looked up in total surprise.

"What is the meaning of this?" the president demanded.

"I have something I'm going to tell you, Mr. President," he answered coolly. "Mr. Greenberg here is to provide proof of our conversation. That goes for you too, Rizzuto. I'm sure you were in on it as well."

"How dare you talk to me with that tone," Collins said in an angry voice. "I'm the president of the United States."

I think not for long, you pathetic miscreant.

He leaned over the desk that separated them, looking Collins in the eye, and slammed a sheet of paper down on top.

"You'd better read this very carefully and act on it immediately," he remarked almost casually. "You have until noon tomorrow. Then we go public."

He turned around and strode out with Greenberg right behind.

* * *

Day Eleven—*AP midday news—President Collins stunned not only the nation but the world today. In a live broadcast from the Oval Office this morning at 10:00 a.m. eastern, the president announced that he would be resigning his position with his last day in office being at the end of this month. The president said that he let the country down in the handling of the monetary crisis that has caused such a disruption in the banking sector. He was flanked by Anthony Rizzuto who also made a single statement that he too would be tendering his resignation. No other comments were made by either individual, and since there were no reporters present, the public announcement ended as quickly as it had started.*

*   *   *

Conclusion

"It sure was good of Mills to arrange for us to get a little extra time off," Doug said. "And an all-expense, one-week vacation for the four of us to Hawaii before you and Mary head on out—well, you can't beat it."

"I'm sure he was very persuasive when he talked to Mark," replied Jonathan. "Mary, did I tell you that after he chewed me out for doing the things I did, he turned around and offered me and Doug jobs working as analysts for the CIA?"

"Oh, really," she answered. "And your answer?"

"Well, I looked at him and said it was like this. Doug and I deal with bad people and sleazes all the time, but as of yet, we haven't had any of them threaten our lives or that of our families, so I told him I'd have to take a rain check. Doug said the same. He just laughed but said he might be calling us for some advice anyway."

"Well, I'm glad you did. Anyway, it's been a very interesting start to the cruise," remarked Jamie. "We're barely half an hour out of port when we see that President Collins is resigning."

"Good riddance to bad rubbish," Jonathan said.

"Oh, I'm sure he had a little help in making his decision," Doug remarked with a meaningful glance toward Jonathan.

"Something tells me that these guys aren't telling us everything they know," commented Jamie.

"You never did like him, did you?" Mary said.

"He's a leader in the Democrat Party," Jonathan replied with a disgusted look, "which makes him a Socialist. He's also an Arab sympathizer. He wants to negotiate with the terrorists. I prefer we kill 'em."

"Pretty strong words," said Doug.

"Not really. The basic tenets of Socialism are big government, a huge welfare system, big taxes, and an ever-expanding intrusion into your private life. The only difference between that and Communism is that in Socialism they control business. In Communism, they own it. You may recall that our government now owns 60 percent of General Motors. It won't be long until they're telling GM what cars they can make."

"It sounds like maybe you ought to run for president yourself and fix everything," laughed Doug.

"A lot of good it would do," sneered Jonathan. "No one in the Republican Party has got the backbone to stand up to the media. They're all a bunch of spineless jellyfish. We don't have any conservatives up there anymore. Do you realize that if we had forty-one senators with the guts to do it, we could shut down the government if they wanted to? The first thing I would insist on is a repeal of the Sixteenth Amendment and replace with a 10 percent national sales tax, but no one's going to go for that because it will take away their precious power. You've heard the analogy about the frog and the pot of water. As far as I'm concerned, the United States has become the frog."

"I think we probably should get off the politics and try to enjoy the remainder of the cruise," said Mary. "Otherwise, Jonathan's going to have a coronary."

"Agreed," nodded Jonathan. "I've said my piece. Not another word on the subject."

*　　*　　*

Three weeks later, Jonathan sat across from the pastor of the church somewhat uncomfortably.

"Jonathan, it's good to see you again," he smiled. "It's been a while, hasn't it?"

"Too long," agreed Jonathan.

"I trust you and Mary had a nice vacation," he said. "Mary was hoping you two could iron out a few things. Plus we miss you leading our fourth graders."

"I'd say we were able to take care of the majority of our major problems," said Jonathan.

"I'm glad to hear that," Pastor Hart smiled.

Jonathan paused.

"Is there something else you wanted to ask me?" the minister asked him. "You seem a little preoccupied."

"Well, with the way things have been going lately, doesn't it seem that the end-time is near?"

Pastor Hart laughed. "It could, but you know the scriptures as well as most. No one knows when that day will be. If they claim they do, then they're lying. He said he will come as a thief in the night. But I will guarantee you one thing. When he does come, it will be *just as He said.*"

*   *   *